THE STORYBOOK
CORONER

A.J. SCHAAR

First published in 2023
By Black Chicken Unlimited Imprint
ISBN: 979-8-218-31518-4

CHAPTERS

Chapter I.

LONG, LONG AGO

She was the most beautiful woman in the Universe.

He had just grown a moustache.

Once upon a time, and at the *same* time, they were both in the very same field. A craggy sort of place, but green. It smelled like decomposing. Not a bad smell, not a rotting smell. A decomposing smell like growing things. Like plucky little sticky things clawing their way up through the ground, through the roots of trees. A rutty smell, like goats had rubbed hard against it.

Many, many years later even, neither one could imagine why they would have gone there. 'I hadn't even brought a book with me' she would ponder to herself. Not that it was a bad place, but why on earth had she gone?

He at least had some excuse. He was a goat herder. He loved his work. You may think that goat herding would be dull, but not to him. He was the sort of man who regarded the extraordinary as being commonplace. And the other way around.

Like this.

He had met any number of gods. At this time, of course, most of them were Greek. A lot of them hadn't been created yet. But there were Norse gods and Egyptian gods and Aboriginal gods. Pagan. You know, the long, long ago type of god, when they would still hang out on earth. Classic vintage. Well, he'd be talking to a god, and the god would usually end up talking about something pretty extraordinary. Thor might start chatting about how he was '**the storm.**' Or how he killed Thriazi the mind-reading giant and tore out the eyes of Allvaldi's son and ground them into the black heavens.

One time Thor even announced that someday he'd have a day of the week named after him. Just like that, '*someday I'll be a day of the week,*' and he sipped his mead. What makes *that* extraordinary is that they didn't even have 'weeks' yet, that's how long ago this was. But he was right, as gods *always* prefer to be:

Thor's-day.[1]

At any rate, when a god says extraordinary things like that, you can't really *do* anything about it, which is pretty commonplace.

---

[1] True, from the Old English, Thunresdæg.

But if someone says something like, 'we're out of milk, would you remind me to get some?' or, 'why the hell won't this damn thing work? I followed the directions *exactly* goddamn it!' or, 'could I borrow your finger while I tie this knot?' well *those* are things you can really *do* something about, which is pretty extraordinary.

You can really herd goats.

Even so, there was no special reason why he was in that field. He might have herded his goats anywhere, but there he was. It was so quiet, he imagined he was the only one there (and so did she). He was stretched across the ground on a checkered picnic blanket. He was a long, thin man – so long that he couldn't fit on the blanket all at once. He was just about to enjoy his sandwiches.

She had just finished eating one before she came round that little scarp,

And he saw her.

And she saw him.

And they were perfectly still.

And the whole world was silent.

Then she said, 'I like your moustache.'

And he stood and he said, 'Thanks.'

Because what do you say at a time like that? What can you possibly say? There she was, the most beautiful woman in the Universe, a billowing, immaculate gown, standing there just steps from him, admiring his moustache... Everything about this was extraordinary as he had never known it could be. She was Extraordinariness herself. And he'd like to do something about it.

So he said, 'Would you care for a sandwich?'

And she said, 'I just had one.'

So he said, 'Oh?', and she nodded, 'But one should never turn down a sandwich,' he said.

She smiled the dearest smile in the Universe.

She took a step towards him....

Then the ground beneath her exploded.

Chapter 2.

HIM

His name is Maximilian Asterisk.

He didn't remember how he came to be standing on the very edge of the chasm, looking down into absolute darkness, but there he was. He was silent - he couldn't call out to her. He didn't even know her name. He thought about jumping in after her, but he didn't know if she was down there. Maybe she'd been blown up into the clouds, or blown into a million pieces. She could be anywhere! Or nowhere, anymore. No blood or body to be seen. Just this abyss that, despite the calm afternoon sun, was totally and uniformly of blackest black. So he just stood, deathly white, limp, at the very, very edge, looking into it.

'What have you got there then?' from out of nowhere and from directly behind Maximilian came a friendly, hearty voice, and Maximilian, startled, fell.

'No you don't' said the voice, and Maximilian was grabbed by a powerful hand, and just as suddenly as he fell, he was again on solid ground. Poor Maximilian's heart was whiplashed. He gave the pit a stern look (as though the pit cared), and then turned with a kinder eye to his rescuer. Standing before him was a goat-man. Maximilian blinked. No, it's a goat-man. He had the face of a rogue, the arms of an Adonis, from the waist down he was an animal. He smelled pungently of earth and sex both freshly turned and stale, and at that moment, was happily scratching his arse, really digging in. Maximilian liked him immediately, and with great tenderness.

'Pan' said the goat man shaking hands. 'You're lucky I was here, mate, you don't want to fall in there. You know what that is?' Maximilian shook his head. 'That's a hell hole that is. That's what I call it anyways. Hades hole you could call it. But have you ever *been* to Hades?' Maximilian shook his head. 'Well. It's Hell.'

Pan took a seat near the mouth and peered down. 'Giddy prick!' he shouted down it. Maximilian shakily sat down next to Pan, who smiled at him and repeated sweetly, 'He's a giddy prick.' Maximilian squinted questioningly. 'His name's Hades right? The giddy prick in charge of Hades. He named the bloody place after himself. I told him, that's going to be bloody confusing, that's the stupidest thing I've heard in an age. And do you know what he said?' Maximilian shook his head. 'Piss off, that's what he said, and then he sort of *preened*. And do you know why he said that?'

'Because he's a giddy prick?' Maximilian ventured, dazed.

'That's exactly right. Exactly.' He shouted down the hole, 'SEE? EVEN-sorry, what's your name, mate?'

'Oh, Maximilian Asterisk.'

'EVEN MAXIMILIAN ASTERISK HERE KNOWS THAT YOU'RE A GIDDY PRICK, YOU GREAT, SILLY MONSTER YOU!' Pan turned and smiled wanly at Max, 'My old man, Hermes he's called, well he's Zeus's messenger, right. You've heard of Zeus? He's the one that's **Lord of the Sky**, the one with the ruddy great thunderbolt. Oh, very impressive yes, he can arm-wrestle all the other gods at once and win. Breezing. Not that he does much except chase skirt behind Hera's back, but you can't help but love the guy. At any rate, my old man works for him, *and* for the git down there. Leads the dead there, that's him part-time. I could tell ya stories... I'm not boring you, am I?'

Maximilian shook his head.

'Well I'll tell you. Zeus, he's on top of that mountain there in Olympus, he's with the Muses, he's with the Graces, he's with the Goddesses, each one sexier than the last. That's living I say, that's healthy living. Hades now, he's down there, underground, in all that darkness. His chosen companions? Well, he keeps this hulking great three headed dog with snakes coming out of it. For a pet. Cerberus. Curby he calls it. He's down there playing cards with Sleep and Death and the Furies. And if you haven't met any of them, let me tell you, they're right fecks. I feel for the ferryman down there, I do, Char he's called, he's a sport really.

Poor guy, paddling about all day taking money from dead folks, and the ones that can't pay all wandering up and down the shore, *moaaan*ing and taking cheap shots at him. Terrible line of work. Poor Char. Even the rivers down there are for shite. You've got your river of *woe*, your river of *lamentation*, and what else, er, *fire*, somehow, and, oh, *unbreakable oath*, and damn I can never remember the last one... It'll come to me... Oh! The River of *Forgetfulness*. Ha.'

'She's down there.' Maximilian breathed.

'Who's down there?' Pan leaned in and whispered.

'I don't know.' Maximilian whispered.

'Love at first sight.' Pan said loudly. 'I knew it. I knew it - just like that. I've been in love at first sight, oh, what would it be, I dunno I've lost count, thousands of times now. At least.' He leaned in to whisper again, 'I made the Moon once.' He smiled, 'now what do you think of that?'

Maximilian was staring into the pit.

'Don't you dare.' Said Pan. 'Look. You're not a god are you?'

'I'm a goat herder.'

'You are? You're kidding. I love goat herders, wonderful people, some of my favorites. I knew I liked you! But this is what I'm talking about. You're mortal. That means, you can go down there, but you can't get back out. That's old Curby's joy in life, the stupid brute. Worse than him, Hades himself. Now if he took your woman down there, he wants her. He's not supposed to make these bloody hell holes. Look at it, just sitting there, right there, right out in the open, pretty as you please. It's reckless endangerment is what it is! Not that he cares. But Zeus will. Look, the point is: if you go in there alive, you're not coming back with her. You're not coming back, period.'

'Is she still alive?'

'I doubt it. Even if you take your body with you, being dragged down to hell is bound to have some effect.'

'Then I'll die, and I'll join her.'

'No. If you die, you'll be his. And he's not going to care about your great, beautiful love at first sight. And if she loves *you*? He'll torture you. He'll annihilate you. And do you know why?'

'Because he's a giddy prick.'

They both turned to look into the hell hole. Pan put a comforting arm around Maximilian.

'We'll have a good think about it. I know a few people... Tomorrow, we'll put our heads together, and we'll come up with a terrific plan. One for the books, alright? But not now. Now, we need to get really drunk. Come on then, up you get, mind your step there, Maxi.'

Chapter 3.

HER

Her name is Persephone.

She was hurtling at high speed through the dark, smoothly and silently. She looked back to the patch of light. Far away, she saw a figure leap into view, or did she, and then it all vanished, was swallowed up by what seemed like an incredible distance. She held her own hand and faced forward.

Great black stallions, perhaps dozens of them, were flying the comfortable black chariot she was now seated in through the air. Beside her, driving them, an old man, incredibly big and very strong, shabbily dressed with a scruffy beard. He turned to her, *astonishing* eyes. He smiled at her as though in commiseration, 'Well now,' he said, 'this is either an awkward situation, or the extraordinarily memorable beginning of a friendship. I hope it's the latter.'

Persephone wasn't sure what to say to this. Why should she be friends with her kidnapper, she thought.

The man watched her. 'Why should you be friends with the villain who is even now in the process of kidnapping you? A very good question. For two reasons. The first, you are being taken to Hades, there to be Queen of all the Dead, where I shall be one of your loyal employees, and to be a professional friend to your staff, when and if appropriate, is just good business sense, it's better for everyone. The second, *this* is *not* my idea. There is a third reason I believe, and even a fourth, but I'll leave that for you to decide.'

This politic speech from her enormous, unkempt abductor seemed at such odds to Persephone that she was quite taken aback - and she was fairly stunned already.

'But where are my manners? My name is Charon. Will you do me the honor of calling me as my friends do, simply Char.' His great hand enveloped her own.

'Persephone' she said, surprised that she had, and that it had sounded calm.

'Persephone,' said Char looking at her intently. 'Charmed. Shall I tell you something?'

She nodded.

'I've seen so much that now I can *see* what I'm looking at. And when I look at you... Believe me when I say how sorry I am to take you to Hades. But I think he'll be getting more than he bargained for with you. Yes, I think there's a very good chance that Hades won't know what hit it.'

Her beautiful eyes squinted her confusion.

'Ah,' said Char, 'The King of the Dead, your surprise fiancé, is named Hades. He named his realm after himself. It was originally called the Underworld for the obvious reason that it is Under the World. It has been pointed out to Hades that his new choice of name causes constant confusion, but he is not the sort of man who likes to have his choices questioned. For my own part, I think the irritation it provokes amuses him. But then, he is violently unpredictable; I may well be wrong.

'The last thing I want is to cause you distress. Well, any *further* distress. And, I am sure you'll have him wrapped around your finger. But permit me to give you this word of caution. Hades can be kind, generous, remarkably so, even on a whim... But please, be on your guard. I mean this kindly, as your first friend here.'

Persephone nodded, hugged herself and bit her perfect lip. She was determined not to cry. She wouldn't cry, she wouldn't cry. She wouldn't beg to be taken back. She wouldn't be afraid. She would make the best of a goddamn god*damn*it awful situation. I mean, it's heartbreakingly unfair to meet the love of your life the moment before you're dragged to hell, but those are the breaks sometimes. She didn't want to be Queen of the Dead, married to what was starting to sound like a psychopath for a husband whom she had never laid eyes on before, but some days are just like that. No use looking back. Right? Right.

She looked back to where the light had been.

She *knew* he was standing there, right there where she was looking... but she couldn't see him. And she knew he couldn't see her looking right back at him, *so* wanting to see him.

It was too much.

'One should never turn down a sandwich' she said, and Persephone cried.

Chapter 4.

HADES

The chariot was suddenly still. A bright, dirty light snapped, replacing the blackness. The great, charging stallions were as unmoving as an unplugged carousel. Persephone dried her eyes, wiped her nose with her wrist. It felt frozen, looked marble. She peered over the edge of the chariot.

Far below, she had never seen so many people. They were dressed raggedly. Upon seeing her, they began to cheer, unenthusiastically, 'yayyy.' They were assembled in an enormous courtyard. Beyond, in shadows, a structure so massive she could not see its end. So many gates, too many doors to ever count. Everything black, black stones, black panels, black metals... Even black rivers stretching around it, across the land, pooling into black lakes like glass.

Then the crowd began to part, making way for a single figure. In black. It beckoned towards her, an elegant gesture. Chariot, horses and all began to descend, slowly, lingeringly. The figure was a man's of average build. His features were hard but handsome. Tragedy, was what struck Persephone. The way he stood, the way he breathed, in the corners of his eyes; as though he were smiling through unspeakable sadness. She didn't notice the chariot's landing, didn't hear what Char whispered to her. They were face to face now. The figure gently opened the door, offered her his hand, and she took it.

'Pleasant trip?' he asked. She raised her eyebrows, nodded. 'Oh good. I'm glad,' an awkward pause, 'May I?' She nodded. Rather than helping her down, he took her face firmly in his hands, caressed her cheek. 'You're very beautiful. Did you know that?' She shrugged delicately.

'Oh, don't give me that. You are. You know you are.' He tapped the tip of her nose; she smiled. 'I love you.' She looked down. 'I adore you.' His hands moved to her throat and tightened. 'Look at me.' She did. 'This long neck. These shoulders, these...fingers, these wrists. I love you. Will you make me the happiest of men, and be my bride - my Queen?' A pause. She looked, transfixed, on him... She nodded. 'Oh darling,' he moaned and kissed her.

'I'm Hades by the way' he said, helping her down, 'Could you come stand by me please? Thank you.' He turned to address the crowd, 'My people!' he roared, 'May I present to you your Queen! Queen...' he hadn't thought to learn her name.

'Persephone' Char murmured.

'...Persephone!' Hades beamed. The crowd cheered. 'A bit louder, please.' Louder cheering. 'Smile darling' he said under his breath, and Persephone did, beautifully. Flashbulbs went off. 'That's enough. Off you go.' The crowd rapidly dispersed, grumbling under their breath.

'Tsk, they're sweet, aren't they? And they'll do whatever you say. Do you like that? We'll have such fun you and I, *commanding* them. A whole kingdom for you! And a king. A *god*. Did you know that? You'll love getting to know me.'

He placed her arm in his and together they strolled towards a river. 'Now. You look at me, and you see something you've been fighting all your life: Death. You'd like to destroy me, am I right? But you also feel at home, at rest, protected; your deepest fear *adores* you. You want to lie in my arms forever. Don't you.'

Hades watched her intensely. She gave away nothing. He smiled.

'You see this river? This is The River of Forgetfulness.' He ran a hand over her collar bones. 'Now. You're such a soft, sensitive girl, I'm sure you loved many things in your life. Many people. Didn't you.' He watched her.

'You know,' he continued, 'it's a funny thing. *Forgetting* in their death is what most people worry about when they're alive. So I'm told. They're worried that they'll lose themselves somehow in the ether or the *cosmos* or whatever you like to call it. And then they die, and they come here, and they remember everything! And *then*, they all *choose* to forget. *Why* do they all choose to forget? I'll tell you. They don't want to remember anymore. Simple as that. They think of walking through their door and having their loving pet waiting for them. Going out with their friends, talking with their parents, sharing a glass of wine, sitting outside watching the rain, the stars... They think of the love of their life, if they're lucky. But now it's all *gone*. Poof! Like that. And they can't. go. back. Ever.'

Hades paused to observe his effect, but Persephone said nothing. He continued with sardonic charm.

'Oh, sometimes people hold off forgetting for quite a while. They hope to find their friends, their loves here. But Hades is a very big place. And forever's a very long time. So eventually they start to ruin their own memories on purpose, by remembering too much. They want to make that nasty nostalgic hurt of theirs go away. So badly. So they start to remember the arguments they'd forgotten. The sins they'd forgiven. The annoying habits that drove them up the wall... Maybe they're better off without all that, right?

'But *then,* they start to remember the terrible things they've done them*selves*... And they *torture* themselves with what might have been. What they should have done. What they could have had if they'd said something else. How they wasted their Chance.

'Sometimes - rarely, but sometimes - one of them does find one of their long-lost-loves here, and they are overjoyed! Finally, a chance to do it all over, to have them again, and *this time* they'll show them just how much they love them, *this time* they'll be oh so good. So happy.

'But their lost love has no idea who they are. They, have forgotten already.

''What might have been,' they ask themselves. 'What we might have been...' Over and over and over and over. But no going back.

'Forever.'

Persephone looked at the river.

'But you can forget anytime you like! And without a care in the world, you'll be Queen of all this! You'll do just as you wish. Does that please you?'

Still looking at the river, 'Yes.'

Hades was startled to hear this first word from her perfect mouth. He pulled her towards him. 'And do you like your new home, darling?'

She smiled up at him now, the most cunning smile in the Universe, touched her finger to his nose and answered, 'No.'

Chapter 5.

THAT NIGHT

The stars had danced and gone to bed
while Pan and Maximilian spoke,
sometimes softly and sometimes not.
They had made their way through
several skeins of what Pan had called,
'like wine.' As the evening strolled across
the land, the pair talked about how
Persephone, the nameless lady, might be
right now. How they might be able to
rescue her. What might become of
Maximilian and his love.

They agreed that what had happened
was not in fact what's called 'love at first
sight.' It was in fact, as of now, and for
the foreseeable future, the *very* rare, love
at *only* sight.

This, is a sad state of affairs. A love at
first-sight must be assumed to have a
love at *second*-sight, at the very least. But
a love at *only*-sight means exactly that. A

single brush with certainty, never to be met again. Pan was outraged by the very *existence* of love at only-sight, never mind it striking a goat herder. As he drank, he said things along the lines of 'loneliness forevermore, unending regret,' etc. Maximilian said little.

Changing Max's sad fate seemed impossible. Round and round in circles, the pair looked for a chink in the wall, but there didn't seem to be a way over, under or through it. If Maximilian attempts to see the lady while he's alive, he will unquestionably die and be in the power of the cruel and unpredictable lord of the underworld. And, if he attempts to see the lady dead, his existence will most likely be annihilated completely. Almost certainly if it turns out that the lady loves Maximilian in return.

Oh, but this thought bred fresh fear. *Does* the lady love Max in return? Max's affection was so sincere, it hadn't occurred to him to think that... It could easily be that she does not care for him at all. She didn't accept the sandwich when he first offered it, did she? It *looked* like she was going to take it the second time, but who's to say? If she loved him, wouldn't she want to join him, wouldn't she have taken the sandwich? But then again, she did say that she had *just* had one. She's the most beautiful woman in the Universe, who knows how many sandwiches she eats? Thousands? Just one, ever? Who knows. All this about the sandwiches is nonsense anyways. Since when does accepting a sandwich mean you love the person who offered it? It's preposterous.

All the same, Max wished that she had taken the sandwich. 'One should never turn down a sandwich,' Max said quietly to himself.

Pan assured Max that his old man, Hermes, would be able to see the lady the next time he conducted the dead to Hades. When Hermes sees her, he could bring a message to her from Max, and he could find out what *she* wants. It would be a start, at any rate.

If she *does* love Max in return, the pair agreed, they would go to any lengths to save her.

If she does *not*... Well. That was too sad a thought to think much about... Or to ever quite stop thinking about.

Whether she loved him or not, the odds were staggering that anything could ever be done about it. When dealing with immortal gods, it's best to have Time on your side. As Maximilian puts it, 'Alive is not being dead, so you still have a *chance*, with luck, to succeed. Dead is not being alive. You've just got no chance in hell[2]. But, people don't live forever.'

In the dark before dawn Pan was getting emotional. It was probably the 'like wine' talking as he said, 'it's just all so pointless, so. Just let's, let's just try to make the best of a god*damn*it awful situation, and see if the sun comes up tomorrow.'

---

[2] Maximilian is widely credited with coining this expression, or at least he should be.

Dawn rose just after Maximilian and Pan fell to sleep.

A small grey bird, who had listened to their conversation unseen, looked on with thoughtful contempt.

Chapter 6

THE PIGEON

This small, gray bird was to play an instrumental role in the life of Maximilian Asterisk. And, as you will soon know, it has played a very large part in *your* life too. This bird was a pigeon. Or, to be more accurate, a rock pigeon of the family *Columbidae*, as it is called today.

This creature is known to you. They can be found on every continent, in every city, excepting only the driest expanses of the Sahara Desert, Antarctica and its surrounding islands, and in the frozen Arctic of the North.

Pigeons, even feral pigeons, live in a closer proximity to humans than most other birds will allow for. They have even suffered themselves to be domesticated, and found themselves employed throughout the millennia as homing and carrier pigeons. On the whole, they have been so thoroughly useful, that several pigeons have even been decorated for conspicuous bravery in battle.

One notable example is that of the homing pigeon 'Cher Ami,' who, in the course of her duties, was shot in the chest and leg, so that her leg was nearly falling off. Yet despite her painful wounds, she still travelled fully twenty-five miles to deliver her message. Because of this truly splendid act, she saved 194 men of the Lost Battalion of the 77th Infantry Division at the Battle of the Argonne. Verdun, October 1918. Cher Ami was awarded a *Croix de Guerre* Medal by France and a palm Oak Leaf Cluster by the States. Should you wish to pay your regards, she can be found at the Smithsonian's National Museum of American History on permanent display. She's dead of course, but still.

A platoon of pigeons once braved the battlefields of Normandy to deliver vital intelligence to the Allies.

And in 1943, the 'Dikin Award' was created in the UK to honor the military service of animals. On the medal in large script reads, *'For Gallantry'* and beneath, **'WE ALSO SERVE.'** The first three recipients of this award were Winkie, Tyke and White Vision, three pigeons serving with Britain's Royal Air Force for rescuing an Ace flying crew during WWII.

This is all to say there are two things that haven't changed as man has rolled through the ages, from agrarian to iron to enlightenment to whatever one can call today's.

The first is that regardless of circumstance, the pigeon has never ceased being a noble creature. The second is that the clear majority of men despise them. In every language that ever was, man has called pigeon 'flying toilet' and 'rat with wings.' When the society of man lives high and easy, it seeks to exterminate pigeons for dirtying its pristine cities, using any means at its disposal. And when the society of man suffers, it wrings the pigeons' necks to feed its poor and slaves.

Some ornithological psychiatric experts argue that pigeons would not feel these wrongs so deeply were it not for the fact they are essentially *doves*. Doves and pigeons are related so closely that for many species, the only real distinction is their size, doves being somewhat smaller, and stupider.

And yet *doves*, people invite to their weddings. They're asked onto the stage during magic shows for children. Man reveres them as a symbol of Peace. Man coos, 'how sweet' to see a pair of turtledoves. Many would be unafraid to touch a dove's head, and may even treasure the memory for years to come.

And although Pigeons, like doves, also mate for life and raise their young together and even, unlike most birds they even nurse their young with milk, and are *far* more intelligent and adventurous than doves...

The Pigeon is never invited to the wedding. The Pigeon is not to be touched.

The Pigeon fills man with disgust.

So *long* before our story began, *The* Pigeon took its revenge on the World in a manner most final...

Chapter 7

LONG, LONG, LONG, LONG, LONG, LONG AGO

Everything lived forever.

Were this still the case 'long, long ago' when our story begins, our lovers would not be where they are now. There would have been no need for Hades to rule the underworld, since there would be no need for an Underworld. And even if Hades had kidnapped the lovely Persephone regardless, and carried her off to regions undreamt, Maximilian would still always be alive, so he would always have a *chance*.

But such is not the case.

So, as it often *is*, to go forward we have to go back. We must visit the most *ancient* of realities - to the Aborigines of the Outback, which were then Nameless lands.

We must go back, back, back to a string of unlikely and uncommonly specific events...

The first gods man knew lived in the Dreamtime. The father-father, creator of creators was called the Great Rainbow Serpent. It created everything simply because it was Perfect. And because it was Perfect, everyone loved it.

There was another god in the form of a snake in the Dreamtime: His name was Bobbi-Bobbi, and he loved mankind very much.

In those days, man lived on water alone. But Bobbi-Bobbi loved mankind so much, he wanted to give them *more* than just what they *needed*. So he gave them flying foxes to hunt, and boomerangs to hunt them with.

If you're unfamiliar with the creature, a flying fox is a kind of fruit bat, belonging to the megabat suborder *Megachiroptera*. They are the *largest* bats in the world with a wingspan measuring nearly five feet. And as the name suggests, their head looks rather like that of a fox. Fossils from long, long, long, long, long, long ago (at least 35 million years ago to give you an idea) show that that flying foxes then were *exactly* like flying foxes today.

Draw what conclusions you will.

The boomerang, you probably know, is an equally curious thing: A curved stick that flies the way you *don't* throw it. The boomerang is the oldest known means of heavier-than-air, man-made (serpent-invented) flight. The first depictions of boomerangs occur 50,000 years ago (but *we* know it was longer ago than that).

In any case, Bobbi-Bobbi gave mankind flying foxes and boomerangs, and the people were *very* happy.

But there was one man who wasn't grateful. He thought to himself, 'If the gods can give us these uncommonly specific gifts, I bet they're holding out on us. I bet they've got all kinds of great things in the Dreamtime that they're just not *giving us*. If I could see through the clouds to where they go, I bet I could find a way to steal it for myself. Why should they have what I can't have?'

So he went to a friend of his who was a really good boomerang thrower (everyone said so, *and* how nice he was) and asked him to throw one so far that it would cut a hole in the clouds. But his friend said, 'That is not a good idea.'

And the man asked why, and his friend said, 'Because the gods are there in the clouds, and I do not want to hurt one by accident. That would be bad.'

So the man said, 'Oh, well then, if you're too *scared*, just forget about it.'

And this made his friend feel small, and so he was angry, and he said, 'Me? I am not scared of anything. I will show *you*!' And he threw the boomerang at the clouds as hard as he could. And it just so happened, he threw right at the spot where Bobbi-Bobbi was resting.

The boomerang crashed through the cloud and then crashed back towards earth again, frightening the generous-hearted snake. After the boomerang had left, Bobbi-Bobbi wished that he had thought to catch it. But because he didn't, the boomerang came hurtling back at high speed towards the friend who had thrown it, and it killed him.

Accidents do happen, so this was not the first death on earth. But until that fateful day, the Moon - a happy and horny god - had always administered magic water to the dead, which brought the dead back to life.

But *this day*, a small, gray bird saw its opportunity, and took it. You know why The Pigeon, ancestor of all pigeons, held the human world in contempt. Before the boomerang thrower could be raised from the dead, The Pigeon SPOKE.

When The Pigeon concluded, the Moon and Bobbi-Bobbi admitted that although they still loved mankind, all that The Pigeon had said was true.

So the man in his smallness remained dead. The ungrateful man walked away.

And from that day forth, the Moon never gave its magic water again. One by one, each living thing died without resurrection.

Not without hope...

But when it comes to the Everything, Forever, Every Direction through Space Time and Every Dimension There Can Ever Be, Mama Hold On Tight Now **ALL**, hope is sissy stuff.

Chapter 8.

A SECRET

Maximilian woke in the afternoon sun to see the backlit figure of a bird on his chest, close to his face, looking at him.

The bird said gravely, 'I have seen things.' Maximilian rubbed his bleary eyes, 'I have seen everything that does not change.' Maximilian waited, 'I have seen you. I, am The Pigeon.' Thunder rumbled in the cloudless sky.

The bird nodded significantly and flapped to a nearby boulder. Max sat up, and the bird continued rapidly, and hushed, 'I should not say what I am about to say. I have sworn otherwise - but upon myself. I will not stand aside when love is helpless. I will tell you A Secret. You, must do the rest.' Again, thunder rumbled.

Again, Maximilian nodded. The sun shone cheerfully; it seemed out of place.

'This, is A Secret.' The Pigeon said,

'You know it.

'Every Creature loves something with such joy that they Believe in it. This Love is Magic. There are as many Beliefs as creatures, and many more besides; Beliefs for lovers, friends, callings, dreams and everything that ever was or will be that is Good. Belief is a *Way* to The Secret.

'You must be *careful* with this Magic. Once, it brought only bliss, but it was torn long ago, and now it's Magic is unpredictable, dangerous. It can make that which is senseless. Go in peace. The pictures that hang on the wall of a stranger are always sacred.

'Know what *you* Believe in. The voice in your head that laughs far away, that voice is fear.

'You must use all the courage you have and all the courage you have not, and you must Know what you Love. Be as daring you may. To Know is to live beyond fear. But to live beyond fear, you must *first be fearless*.

'See what the air is with your eyes. It is everywhere. Be brave enough to Know what you are capable of. The Secret is the same for every creature, but each Way to it is different. The Way you find The Secret, makes you who you are.'

The Pigeon cocked his head and fixed Maximilian with a birdly stare.

'You love the nameless lady. You love what she is.'

Maximilian agreed, 'she is *extraordinary*.'

Pigeon flapped his wings three times. Then he said, 'Think not, 'I *hope* I love her,' nor, 'I *believe* I love her. Think, Know, 'I *know* I love her.' Let there be no doubt or fear.

'This, is a Spell. If you are brave enough to conjure it, you will understand.

'This, is A Secret. It is known to all, but cannot be told. Understand. Each is his own, the same. Find who *you* are.' A gust of wind blew over them.

Maximilian nodded to the Pigeon and looked to the ground. He looked in stillness. His breathing became shallow, then imperceptible. His expression was stoical and deeply sad. But then, his face broke into a radiant smile, and his eyes were full of tears. His moustache turned every color in the rainbow, and the rest of him followed suit, even the threadbare robes he wore. Then in a flash of light, Maximilian Asterisk disappeared without a trace.

Silence fell.

Then, 'What was *that*?!' Pan exclaimed, 'You there, Pigeon, what have you done with my mate, the goat herder?'

The Pigeon cooed innocently and hopped off the boulder, heading away.

'Oho' Pan grimaced, 'don't play me for a fool, please. I just woke up, and my head's fit to split, but that only makes my hearing *even* keener - I know I heard you talking to Max. So you'd bloody well better start talking to *me* now, mister. What just happened here with the lights and the colors and the...?' Pan was at a loss.

The Pigeon ignored him.

'You know, I was in the middle of something with him.'

The Pigeon ate an insect.

'Alright. Okay. I've about had it with this, sir. Something *weird* just happened, and *you* were running the show. I heard you. Don't deny it. Hey, look at me,' The Pigeon did, 'Don't you bloody well deny it.' Pan continued, standing before the bird, 'I don't understand, I mean... I don't understand what just happened here, and I'm getting a little bit upset about it now. I'm talking to a pigeon. So please. Tell me: what just happened.'

The Pigeon looked back to the grass and continued to walk.

'You know, I don't want to threaten you,' Pan said, 'but I would like to draw your attention to the fact that I'm at least *twice* as big as you are.'

Thunder shook the ground. Pan squinted at the sunny sky. He had to hand it to the bird, he was impressed; that was a pretty slick trick.

Then Pigeon spoke. 'You cannot threaten me. *I*, am The Pigeon.'

Lightning tore from the sky and split the tree Pan had been lying under. Pan made a dart away as a great limb fell.

'Alright, I can take a hint, mate! I'm sorry. I didn't mean no harm,' Pan was apologetic, but there was something about this that just tickled him, too. You never think these things are going to happen when you wake up in the morning. Pan gave The Pigeon a conciliatory smile, 'But can't you tell me please, *Oh Pigeon*, *where* is the goat-herder? Is he alright?'

'More or less,' the Pigeon replied.

'Is he with the lady?' Pan asked.

'No.' The Pigeon said with finality, and hopped away.

'Wait!' Called Pan, 'Can't you tell me where he is?'

The Pigeon halted, and flapped its wings with impatience, and a wind rose from them. Then a voice in the wind came saying, *'he is on his Way, somewhere else.'*

The Pigeon was rising now, Pan called after it, '...Could you be more specific?'

'You must find your own Way there,' the voice in the wind seemed to be all around, and The Pigeon at length flew straight into the sun.

Pan watched it disappear. Then, 'that,' he said, 'is a strange way to wake up. I... love it.'

He scratched himself. Then he spied Max's goats. 'Poor goats,' he said, 'no one to tend to them now. Well. A good deed for the day is in order.'

So Pan went over to the flock and fucked several of the goats, to everyone's mutual satisfaction. Then he spread his arms wide, 'Be free!' he proclaimed to the unmoving goats. And with that, he jauntily set off to see his Da.

He didn't know where Max was, but did know where to find the lady.

Chapter 9.

THE MASTER THIEF

'Oy, you lot! Don't make me turn this train around...' Hermes, the conductor was shouting into a moaning passenger car. 'Quiet down back there, I warned you! Alright then, that tears it. We're going *right* back to a land of the living.'

Cheers erupted from the train car.

'Oho, you'd like that, wouldn't you. Well now. I didn't say *which* land of the living, now did I.'

The train compartment fell silent. 'What does that *mean*?' whispered a voice within, '*exactly*' said another, '*shh*.'

And then only the sound of the train could be heard.

'That's more like it,' the conductor smiled, 'Now then, next stop,' he barked,

'Hades.' Hermes laughed to himself.
You've got to laugh when you can. Then
he pulled the train's whistle a few times
in a celebratory way. Muffled groans
from the train compartment behind.
Hermes laughed to himself again.

Hermes was a short god, but very thick
set. He didn't look like the sort of god
you'd want to insult. Not that you
should ever really insult *any* god. That's
just not a good idea, you know that.

An impressive figure, yet Hermes
usually wore an expression of sheer
good-natured forgiveness. Hermes had a
special place in his heart for trespassers,
thieves and tricksters. He loved them.
And goat herders. So when Pan had
related the story of Max and the
nameless lady ('It's just too bleeding *sad*,
Da') he felt deep sympathy. 'Son,' he'd
said, 'There's no way a mustachioed goat
herder is going to get done over by Uncle
Hades on *our* watch. ...He's such a giddy
prick.'

'He is, Da,' Pan had agreed, 'He's a giddy prick.'

'He is.'

'He is, yeah.'

At this moment, Hermes is conducting the train from the mortal world to the underworld - the *Undiscovered Express*. It's a sleek machine for its time. It would seem old fashioned to us now. More like trains from the 1920's. Wood. Brass. The dinner car had a very beautiful bar, Hermes had made sure of that. Elegant glasses to hold. Mirrors and candlelight and mahogany. West Indian mahogany, from the Caribbean. It still smelled like the breeze there if you really sat back and breathed it in.

It can't be said that Hermes *uncrafted* all this so the souls he conveyed could make their crossing in style and ease-

He just liked it.

Are you wondering why Hermes *uncrafted* the train? That's understandable. Uncraftsmen were much in demand at the time, though they're few and far between now. *Uncrafting* is the only way to build a bridge between realms. Then you *unchart* a course to where you want to go, set off on that course to where you're not going, and you end up just where you should be.

Subtle business, being the conductor.

This trip he was especially focused. He was looking forward to meeting the nameless lady. Sounded like she must be a helluva looker. And although he hadn't met the goat herder, he hoped he could do him a good turn. *Wherever* he was... 'Hmm,' Hermes thought to himself, 'slim odds on this one... But think of the return! We're talking *big* numbers here.' Hermes liked long shots and dark horses. Liked them very much.

Yes, he'd see what was what with this love at *only*-sight. Though he wasn't looking forward to seeing Hades.

Chapter 10.

WELCOME TO HELL

The train pulled up and stopped at the platform. The At-Hand Central Station[3] was open air. It's built *just* on the inside of the gates. The very edge of Hell. It's an impressive view. When you first arrive, you, the train and the platform, are all suspended in space. There's a dim, angry light ahead of you. And between you and the light, is the river Lethe. You board the boat directly from the train, after you pay your fare.

'Honestly,' Hermes often thought here, 'Hades is just *so* badly governed. Other afterlives find ways so that the dead don't have to pay. Hades is a majorly developed afterlife, why can't they figure out something like that here?' Hermes shared his son's negative views of the place. *Zeus* had the right idea. Poseidon

---

[3] For The End is At Hand.

too, 'but have you ever tried to sleep with a fish? Poseidon can *keep* it.'

Many souls in tattered, black uniforms were busy now, ushering the arrivals out of the train and into queues for the boat.

'Bloody ridiculous way to treat the poor rotters.' Hermes thought, 'they make them throw away their drinks on the train before they can get onto the platform, so they'll have to buy new drinks while they wait for the boat. Money thrown after money. So selfish. No way to treat the dead.'

'Hey Herm?' came a funny, froggy voice, 'Fix ya a gin ricky, Herm? Nice and sweet, just like ya like it?'

'No Bert, thanks, but not right now. I've got to see the giddy prick.'

'Oh, Hades you mean, Herm? He *is* kind of a giddy prick, isn't he. He is like that, now that you say it, yeah Herm.'

'Yeah Bert, yeah - he is.'

Bert is the brakeman of the Undiscovered Express. He liked his job. He liked its importance. 'Big job, stopping a train, need a big man to do it,' he would say to himself sometimes when he looked in a mirror. Bert was not especially clever. But he was keen. He liked the signaling part of the job, signaling back and forth with Herm - 'And Herm's the *conductor*' he would think, 'he runs the *whole* thing. I run the brakes, but he run the *whole* thing. He really is the son of Zeus.'

Yes, Bert liked his job.

'Alright mate,' said Hermes, 'I'll be seeing you in an hour or so. Get into trouble for me, that's the lord's work you know,' Hermes smiled and clapped a hand on Bert's shoulder, 'Get into plenty of trouble, now. Just try to make sure that you never get caught. Ah! It's the joy of me heart.'

'Alright boss,' Bert was always a little sad to see Herm go, 'See ya when I see you. Bye for now.'

Hermes stepped onto the platform with a brave stride. He knew Bert was already missing him. Hermes shook his head, 'tsk, a *sweet* guy.' Then he straightened the wings of his sandals and flew into the commuters' Terminal of At-Hand Central Station. He'd called ahead to hire a chariot. One learns these things when one travels to the Underworld often. Always call. You'll never get one otherwise. The lines are *ridiculous*. You might as well walk.

The carriage driver was foreign to Hermes. Isn't that always the way... Hermes knew it was his own fault for not learning more languages. Well, he *knew* that, but he also knew he wasn't going to do anything about it. *And* he knew that probably nobody was working on tailoring the Underworld just for *his* convenience. He knew with almost certainty, the thought hadn't even occurred to anyone to do so. Probably, not even *one meeting* had been held, or even scheduled. Or ever would be. He knew all these things, yet still, he felt resentful about it whenever inconvenience faced him here in Hades. He wasn't sure why.

Hermes addressed himself to the foreign driver, 'The **Res-i-dence**, please,' he said loudly and slowly. 'You savvy *Res-i-dence*? Good. Thanks, mate.' He sat back, his elbow resting moodily on the window of the carriage. What a view. Black, black, black. Hellogen lighting. Burning rubbish in the streets. Overpriced everything. No minimum wage. Theft and greed in *desperation*, 'not for the joy of it all' Hermes meditated. 'But,' he reasoned, 'it's what you'd expect. Their king is a twisty snot, the poor souls.'

The carriage approached a vast, black marble courtyard. There were armed guards heavily patrolling the perimeter. No one was allowed thru without express permission from the king himself. The carriage stopped and a guard approached, with an air of condescension, and a face of little intelligence. 'Name?' the guard asked.

'Are you *really* going to do this again?' sighed Hermes. He'd known this guard for years.

'Name?' the guard persisted.

'You know my name, Eric.'

'*Eric*, is it?' cross-examined the guard.

'Sure, yes. Although you *know* my name is not, yes my name is Eric.'

Eric the guard stood up and closely read the paper on his clipboard. At length, with the swagger of authority, 'Well, Eric, if that really is your name,' the guard adjusted himself, 'There is no 'Eric 'on the guest list. So just turn around now, and no one needs to get hurt.'

'For Pete's sake, Eric,' Hermes sighed, 'Someday it's not going to be like this, I pray. And I've got an inside line on that. But if you must know, for today, my name is Hermes.' He adopted a grand pose, and tone, 'I, am your king's nephew. Patron of this that and the other. I am the wingéd one. And I called ahead.'

'Sorry, Your Wingédness,' said the guard, consulting his clipboard, 'I'm sorry about that, but you can't be too careful.'

'Oh I don't know about that now, I don't know if you were very careful at all!' twinkled Hermes. 'You didn't recognize *me* - only my name. Now, if I wanted to get in there when I *shouldn't*, I'd have a plan. Maybe I'm actually a murderer named Dillon: I made the real Hermes call ahead at knife point, just before I did him in, disguised myself as him, and then came here myself saying that I, Dillon the murderer, am Hermes, and I called ahead. And *you* just let me thru!'

The guard took a step backwards. It had never occurred to him that someone would say they were someone they weren't... The clipboard had always seemed so *reliable*. He felt like he'd been living a lie. 'Listen,' said the guard, 'maybe you should just wait here until I can find somebody to confirm your identity, sir.'

'Oh there's no need for that, because I've got the perfect solution for you! Why don't you,' Hermes fixed the guard with a confident smile, 'Ask me something that only the *real* Hermes would know.'

'Good idea!' said the guard, 'Alright then… What kind of thing should I ask you?'

'How about this. Why not ask me what my favorite vegetable is, and see if I get it right?'

'Good idea,' said the guard, happy and proud to be doing such due diligence now, 'Whoever you are,' he said, 'what's your favorite vegetable?'

'Cauliflower' said Hermes without a moment's hesitation; it had that ring of truth.

'…Is that right?'

'Yes it is. I should know. It's reminds me of a cloud.'

'Well that's alright then, sir. It's been a pleasure talking with you. I apologize for any inconvenience. I hope you have a good day.' This was something Eric had been taught to say. Exactly those words. Hermes had heard it recited many times.

So Hermes had decided to give the same *reply* every time, word for word. It was their little ritual. Eric would say, 'I hope you have a good day,' and Hermes would gasp, and then lean forward conspiratorially to whisper, 'I read you loud and clear, Wild X. Tango, tango. The minks are on the loose. I repeat: the minks *are* on the loose. Understand?' And the guard would always nod in a way as if to say, 'you can trust me. They don't call me Wild X for nothing,' although he had *no* clue what it meant. But that's ritual for you. It made them each happy, in their different ways.

Concluded, the carriage lurched ahead and they crossed the vast courtyard to the palace. Black, black, black. But then, as they pulled up to the entrance, a red door.

Chapter 11.

SOME DISGUSTING THINGS

The red door opened, and the most beautiful woman in the Universe emerged, in a voluminous antique-looking gown of yellowing white.

'I'm sorry to rush at you like this,' she said, 'but a visitor!' she clapped her hands in delight. 'No one's *ever* visited us.'

'Us?'

'Hades and me,' the lady said, 'we've only just been married.'

'I see,' said Hermes. This lady seemed radiantly happy - he couldn't fathom *why*? This place is Hell! And just think, the poor goat herder will have a broken heart, if he could find the heart to tell him. Or find him.

'Do you like my door?' she asked, breathlessly, and turned to beam at her handiwork.

'I do like it,' said Hermes, 'I like it very much. If only you could work your charms on all the rest of it.'

'Yes,' she beamed, 'It's going to be *marvelous*. Look at this place. Potential *everywhere*. It's all going to be simply the most *divine* old river-Styx-side property for all the souls who come here to enjoy. And it'll be *subsidized*. Major public benefits. When I'm through with this place, it's going to be to *die* for, no matter what you came from. But where are my manners? Please, come in, won't you?' She practically skipped thru the door, the most beautiful woman was afizz. Hermes smiled after her as she disappeared into the dim lighting inside. He shook his head, fixed his hat, bowed his head, and followed suit.

'How long have you been here?' Hermes asked as the red door closed. 'Oh,' she said, 'I couldn't say. There's no time here you know. Or is it that there's *only* time? I forget. Oh, I don't suppose it matters much. If *you* were Time, you wouldn't care what people thought of you; it wouldn't make a difference to what you *were*. Or what you weren't. You *really* wouldn't care if you *weren't*. At any rate, I don't know how long I've been here. Or maybe I forgot.

'Ah. You've had a dip in the river,' Hermes couldn't blame her, but how disappointing... The lady put a hand on his shoulder, she seemed eager to confide something or other, but before another word could pass, Hades appeared at the top of a master staircase (one of *many*), in black. He posed for effect. 'Talking about *me*, darling?'

'No,' dismissed Persephone.

'Oh,' deflated Hades. He sniffed, and began a stylish descent down the stairs. 'Hermes!' he called across the closing distance, 'you're in this realm so often, and I so rarely see you. It's almost like you don't want to see me. I miss you,

you know. It's too bad you couldn't have been here a little sooner; you *just* missed our wedding!' He gestured towards a ballroom far away, its door ajar. Every other door was shut. Through the opening, you could see the lady's touch. Fairy lights twinkled through the darkness of the long corridor. 'Hermes,' Hades had joined them on the landing, 'May I introduce to you my bride, Persephone, now queen of the dead.'

'Persephone,' said Hermes, and kissed her cold hand, 'charmed.'

'Persephone,' Hades continued, 'I'm *sorry* to introduce you to this truly disgusting young man, whose sole merit lies in having the privilege of being *my* nephew: Hermes.'

The lady smiled and said, '*some* disgusting things do an awful lot of good. And *some* are quite amusing. May I ask, which kind are you?'

'I hope, m'lady, that I'm both.'

'Yes, I'm sure you are, sir.'

They liked each other immediately, and with great tenderness.

Hades felt like a third wheel, and he couldn't understand why *that* should be. This was *his domain* after all. 'Well,' Hades said after what seemed like awkward pause to him, 'thanks for stopping by Herm. We're bushed, you can understand, it's been a big day. Don't be a stranger now,' Hades had ushered Hermes back as far as the threshold.

'*Hades*,' the lady's voice was sharp, 'where are your manners?' Hades flinched. She continued, 'Hermes is our guest. A guest enters a home like a flame which must be cooled. And I think...' she got close to Hermes, who had also been startled, 'mm-hmm. Sweet gin rickeys cool this fire.' Hermes nodded. 'Right this way.' She led Hermes by the arm down the dark and endless hall, 'Coming darling?' she called flatly back to Hades, without turning. Their laughter echoed off the walls.

Hades watched them fade away uneasily. He wanted to hurt something. 'You there, boy,' he called too sweetly to a young servant holding a silent butler. The boy put down the ancient silver tray and brush. He wiped his hands on his uniformed pants, several sizes too big. The boy approached and stood at attention, 'yes, my king?'

'... Just what do you mean by *your* king?' Hades snarled, pleased to have found such an easy fight, '*Your* king? And just who do you think *you* are. You work for *me*,' Hades seized the silent butler and brandished it, 'you sweep my *crumbs* for *me*. Come here!' he barked. The boy did, frightened.

Then Hade's whole attitude shifted and he said, 'I am so sorry. I'm just overtired, that's what it is. Do you know that feeling? Of course you do, you slave so hard. Here, here, just so there's no bad blood, have a cigar.'

The boy took the cigar tentatively. 'Thank you very much, sir,' said the boy.

'You like it?' asked Hades, 'then *smile* for me, would you? Come on, it won't hurt you!' The boy cautiously smiled, '*there's* the sun,' Hades crooned. 'Here,' he added, 'let me light it for you,' Hades lit the cigar with his mind. 'This is much better, isn't it?' he asked the boy, who nodded and puffed happily, 'yes I think so too. Much better. Unless... Say, you're not on *duty* are you?' A spasm of panic crossed the boy's face as he nodded. 'Oh *shoot*,' said Hades, 'I was afraid of that. You *know* you're not supposed to smoke on duty. You can get in a lot of trouble for that. Like *this*,' and in a moment the lit cigar was jammed into the boy's eye.

The scream was terrible. It made Hades feel better immediately. In a wave of warmth and compassion now he patted the writhing boy's shoulder and said, 'you should ice that after your shift ends. Here,' Hades palmed the boy a small piece of money, flowing over with feelings of generosity and love for humanity, 'get something you need.' And off he set down the hall to join his

beautiful bride and his sadly humorless
nephew.

Chapter 12.

IT OPENS IN

As soon as they were out of earshot, Persephone stopped and grabbed Hermes' shoulders and whispered, 'Did *he* send you to me? The man with the moustache?'

Hermes was overjoyed to learn the lady's thoughts were with the goat herder, 'In a manner of speaking, he did.' Persephone squealed as quietly as she could. 'I haven't met him personally. My son came upon him just moments after Hades came for you. Your story has made quite an impression.'

'Really?' she breathed, she was almost afraid to ask, but, 'what's his *name*?'

'His name is Maximilian Asterisk.'

'How funny!' she chirruped, 'isn't an asterisk where you put all the things that get left out of a story?' She smiled to herself for a moment, 'I love it,' she concluded.

'He loves you,' Hermes said.

Goosebumps and flutters. A silent dance. The lady's heart was full. 'I love him too.' She said.

'There's just one problem,' Hermes winced - sometimes he hated being the messenger, 'We don't know where he is, he disappeared.'

The boy's scream echoed down the hall.

'He disappeared??' she whispered, but then Hades footsteps approached.

'Hi again,' he said. 'Where's your drink Herm, gin rickey was it? Let's see what we've got. Here we are, the bar's in here...' He struggled to push a large, heavy, dusty door open. A spider scuttled down the wall. Hades crushed it with his heel and smiled. 'Ah, locked. Of course. It's the servants you know, they steal everything that isn't nailed down. But never fear...' he pulled out a ring of crumbling skeleton keys, and tried each of them to no avail. He put his shoulder to the door. Then he gave it a running start, but still the door didn't budge.

'May I try?' said Hermes at length.

Hades, winded, waved for him to give it a try, but looked like he felt skeptically about any success.

Hermes pulled on the doorknob once, and the door swung open. He shrugged at Hades and escorted Persephone into the chamber. Hades followed behind. The first two quickly found chairs, and thanked Hades for bartending. Hades didn't want to make the drinks anymore, so as he did, he chipped the ice really aggressively. The other two chatted, nonchalantly.

'So,' said Hermes, 'It sounds like you've grand plans for this place.'

'Yes,' she replied, 'oh yes. I can't wait.'

'What's your vision?'

'I want to make it like home. Like everyone's home. I think they'd like that. With water features and firesides and fresh air and green earth. Light and color everywhere. The most beautiful colors...' she was enraptured, 'And I'm going to completely overhaul the economy.'

'She's extraordinary isn't she?' Hades came over, drinks in hand, 'ice water for you my dear, and a gin rickey for *you*.'

'That looks good, I'll have one too,' said the lady.

'You don't drink,' said Hades taken aback, '*I* don't, so no one here does.'

'Oh!' she said, '*that's* where we got confused. It's: *you* don't drink. *I* don't alone when no one else does.

'Of course... How silly of me,' Hades was in too poor a humor now to know how to argue that. 'I'll be back in a jiff,' he said and stalked back to the bar. He chipped much more ice than he needed.

While Hades was at the bar, under cover of the murderous ice-chipping, Persephone used her smallest voice, 'I love whispering, don't you?' she said, 'it makes things feel so important. Like this: Maybe there's a way out of here, and maybe there's not. What do you think?'

'What do *I* think?' Hermes whispered back, 'I think you're talking to The Master Thief.'

Persephone smiled, 'I knew that I felt safe with you.'

'*What are we whispering about?*' Hades was looming over them, gin rickey in hand. '*Secret* plans for the place?'

'Yes actually,' Persephone grinned at Hermes, 'It will all be alright.'

Hades looked for a third chair, but had to settle for a dusty ottoman. He pulled it up to the chairs and reached for the water. It was sweaty now. It slipped out of his hand onto the dusty floor. He flew into a fit.

'You know,' he said shaking the spill from his hands, 'While we're talking about it, I don't know with what *money* you're planning to make these *beautiful* changes with. It doesn't make a bit of sense to me that you shouldn't take and keep all the money you can. That's just intelligence. You'd do well to remember that *I* am the King here, and *you* are queen at my pleasure. That's all you are.'

'No honey,' Persephone's sweet voice came rhythmically from the blackness beyond the window. Without opening her perfect lips, she looked at Hades, 'You know,' her disembodied voice had a laugh to it, 'if you only look for caged birds, the free might as well as be invisible!' Her voice flew back out the window, and she sipped her drink. Some spilled down her perfect chin and she giggled at her mistake.

Hades' confusion was *evident*.

This pleased Hermes who adjusted himself in his chair. 'She *is* extraordinary,' he agreed.

He'd like to find a way to help this lady. His boys would want to help too. A good deed for the day is in order...

But how to find the goat herder now?

Hades stalked out of the lounge as though he'd had it with an argument and he was thru with being the reasonable one. This left the lady and the master thief to wonder together, where could Maximilian Asterisk *be*?

Chapter 13.

VALHALLA

Valhalla, land of the valorously slain, has a grand, majestic hall. It is *very* grand, indeed. A place of gleaming, polished wood, and ivory, and steel. It's lit gregariously by merry fires burning above and below. They glint off the armor and swords of the dead living there. It is also home to the Valkyries, no less majestic women; lovers of heroes, daughters of royalty, choosers of these slain.

A place of many rooms. Every room without exception contains one of three things: the brave, the beautiful, or the debauched. Valhalla is seen to best advantage in a room containing all three at once.

There is one particularly remarkable room now. Sitting in an enormous, wooden, dragon-upholstered armchair, is the *owner* of Valhalla, great Odin. He has a remarkable big beard, even in a place famous for them. He has one eye. Two ravens are there, one on his shoulder, one on the armrest; their names are Thought and Mind. They are charged with informing Odin of the whisperings and happenings throughout the twelve realms of Asgard - one of the nine home worlds. They are also Odin's pets. At this moment, Odin is laughing at them as they flap and fail to get at a hunk of bread he is holding out of reach. Truth be told, he might have had a few meads, he is laughing harder than it is funny.

This did not escape the notice of Frigg, Odin's wife, a goddess of marriage, who was luxuriating on the skin of The Terrible Whacking Bear, beside Odin, at a fire. As Odin laughed too hard, Frigg rolled her beautiful eyes.

This did not escape the notice of Freyja, a goddess of sex, war and death, leaning against a wall opposite, coolly examining her fingernails. When she spied Frigg roll her eyes, Freyja laughed. She laughed like dark chocolate - it was sweet but it was bitter.

And *this* did not escape the notice of Freyr, 'The Lord,' twin brother to Freyja, a giver of *pleasure* and peace to mortals. He was sitting near Frigg, stroking his boar, Goldenbristles, who glowed in the dark. He noticed Freyja laugh because he had already been sitting there admiring her in quiet. He often did.

And *none* of this escaped the notice of Loki, the shapeshifting trickster. Although, no one noticed *him*. Loki was unhappily sitting on a stool that he felt too high up on, but there wasn't anywhere else to sit, so. Fine. 'So you're just going to spy on each other and ignore *me*?' Loki asked, 'after all I *went* through just to come and see you?'

Odin was still amused by the ravens, but he tried to look authoritative when he finally turned to Loki, '*After all you went through just to come and see me?*' he asked incredulously. He had a big-bearded, booming voice.

'Yes. I *killed* men to get here.'

'*You killed my* guards, *you* charlatan *of creation, you.*'

'But I told you. I had to.'

'*Because they wouldn't let you in?*'

'I couldn't let them stop me.'

'I told *them to stop you. You've* got to stop *killing my guards. I mean it this time.*'

'You stop telling them to stop me then.'

'*No.*'

'On your own head be it. *You* stop killing your guards.'

'*I'm not. You stop.*'

'No *you.*'

'*No* you.'

Frigg had had enough of this, 'Boys,' she said in her best I've-*just*-about-had-it-now mom-voice, 'you're both to blame here. *Both* of you stop killing guards. Now, I don't want to hear *one* more word on the subject.' Goldenbristles grunted in approval. Frigg had an effective mom-voice for everything. Her mom-voice ran the full spectrum. Her comfort brought bliss, and her damnation destroyed the enemies to her heart. She was very impressive.

Odin and Loki thought so. Odin, because he was *married* to that. Loki, because he killed one of her sons. Long story. Frigg did *not* care for Loki. But he's family, and you know how that can be. You've got to grin and bear it sometimes. As for Loki, he knew he could probably best Frigg in a battle. Or if it came to it, he could turn into a fly and buzz away, quick as he could careen. Still, Frigg put him on edge sometimes. When she said things like, 'not one more word,' with that voice, he got a little nervous.

It was into this divinely tense room that a dashing man walked, sporting an extraordinarily blue-black moustache. He stopped just inside the door, 'I'm sorry to walk in on you like this.' he said, 'But something horrible has happened to your guards.'

Loki snickered and Frigg snorted. The Norse gods studied this man. Goldenbristle sniffed the air.

Freyja bounced herself off the wall she'd been leaning against, and the rest of her bounced too, 'who are you?' she asked with sincere curiosity, there was something *unusual* about him.

'My name' he said, standing straight, 'is Maximilian Asterisk.'

Hi there, hello chimed in the room. 'I'm Freyja,' the goddess introduced herself and shook firm forearms (and the rest of her shook too), 'and this,' she continued, 'is our host, Odin.'

'*What are you doing here?*' Odin said bluntly.

Frigg intervened, 'I'm apologize for my husband. He tortures his guests if they let him talk. I'm Frigg. This is Freyr - *hi* - and that, is Loki.'

Loki smiled with great assurance, 'I'm sure you've heard of me.' He wasn't really sure of that at all, really. This man didn't look like one of theirs. The odds were *slimmm*. But he hazarded this brazen boast, because if it worked, think of the return! We're in big numbers here. The others didn't give it a second thought, no *way* this man had heard of Loki... No bet.

But in fact, Maximilian *had* heard of Loki before. 'You're not the one who shaved poor Sif's head, are you?'

'The same!' crowed Loki, triumphant. The others couldn't believe it.

'No offense,' Freyja said, 'but you don't look like you belong here.'

'How can you tell?' Maximilian asked.

'You're unarmed.' the quintet replied without hesitation. 'I wonder,' Freyja continued, 'how you could have heard of Loki shaving dear Sif's head?'

'Sif's husband told me. Thor. Sometimes I watch his goats. I'm a goat herder.' Thor travelled between the realms on a chariot pulled by two magical goats that could fly.

'On Middle Earth you mean?' Freyr asked.

'Yes.' Said Maximilian. He was glad to be having a casual conversation. He was the sort of man who regarded the extraordinary as commonplace, and the other way around, but the past two days (or was it?) had been exceptional. Chatting like this made everything that had happened to him seem like it would all be alright. He wasn't sure what *had* happened to him...

'*What are you doing* here?' Odin asked, more politely this time.

'I don't know,' Maximilian said.

'*Well* how *did you get here?*' Odin tried.

Maximilian thought. 'I'm not sure.'

'*Is there anything you* do *know that you could share with us?*' Odin leaned his great body forward to the edge of his seat. He expected an answer this time.

'I *do* know one thing, actually.' Maximilian smiled radiantly, and he told them about the lady and how beautiful she was. How he loved her now at only-sight. How her rescue was impossible for him. How he *knew*, that he loved her.

When Max had told his story, there was not a dry eye in the house. The goddesses of love and marriage swooned. The gods of power and pleasure felt this man's wrongs. Even Goldenbristle looked troubledly into the fire. And Loki loved love more than any of them. Loki had been both father and mother. Loki even loved monsters.

'*But,*' Odin continued once they'd collected themselves, '*that doesn't explain how you came to be* here.'

Maximilian stroked his newly blue-black moustache. He wasn't sure himself. He hadn't ever expected to end up in *this* place... But he could only find one way to begin, so Max asked Odin, 'Have you ever met, The Pigeon?'

Murmurs in the room. 'You mean *The* Pigeon?' they asked breathlessly.

'That's who he said he was,' said Max.

'What did he say?' they all leaned in.

And Max told them. He tried to quote The Pigeon as faithfully as possible. It had a stimulating effect on the party. They giggled as though he were telling them he'd bumped into a movie star at a diner, and ended up being treated to a private screening. 'That's so *incredible!*' the gods gushed, 'Can you *believe* it?'

Odin explained, '*this is* very old magic. *Much older than us. We grew up on this stuff.*'

'It's like hearing Bob Marley is back and he's giving a free concert...' Frigg said dreamily. Frigg was blessed with prescience, she had seen *everything* that would ever be. When she said things like this that just didn't make sense, everyone else had gotten into the habit of ignoring her.

Max didn't want to be the one to ask, but, 'Bob Marley?' he asked.

Freyja started from her reverie - *Frigg can see the future!* 'Oh! actually!' she exclaimed, crossing the room to Frigg, apologizing as she went, 'I just tune you out sometimes, and I forget that you're omniscient, I'm sorry hon.' Freyja now addressed the room (who also tuned Frigg out on a regular basis), 'Frigg can see how his story will end!' (*Oh ye-ahs of realization from the room*), 'Frigg, you've seen what will happen to this man and the nameless lady, haven't you?'

'Of course,' Frigg said, 'I have seen everything.'

Max was impressed.

'Tell us?' Freyja thrilled.

Frigg thought for a moment. Then she looked away, 'No,' she said, 'some things cannot be told.'

Oh, they'd heard that before. Every time you've got a really important question to ask it's always, 'some things cannot be told.' They'd all bothered teased and tried to trick Frigg into revealing the future of *Ragnarök* the End of the World, the next Great Battle, the Fate of the *Gods*. But no matter how they tried to ply Frigg, her answer was always, 'it cannot be told.'

But why is *this* simple question in the same category as Ragnarök?

Deepest Mystery also shrouds the future of a goat herder and a nameless lady?

And why would *The* Pigeon, meaning *The* Pigeon, break his oath for this pair?

Love at only-sight should be against the cosmic law, granted. But this... This seemed like *more* than the future of the lovers was at stake. It smelled like Prophesy to them. Of what, they couldn't say. But definitely, yes, Fate perfumed the air around this man. And what of the mysterious lady?

The company contemplated together how curious it was... Only the crackle of the fire could be heard, its light dancing off the surfaces, till Loki, uneasy, broke the silence. 'Somebody say something' he said.

Frigg wanted to help. She was self-conscious about always concealing the destiny of the many worlds from everybody else. She searched her vast future-memory for something she *could* tell them. 'Well. *Someday*,' she offered, hopeful, 'Odin and I are going to be days of the week!⁴' This Oracle concluded, she smiled at them comfortingly, 'There now. That's something now, isn't it.'

The ravens, Thought and Mind screeched.

---

⁴ True. Sometimes Odin goes by Wodin. Wodin's-Day. That's why that *ednes* is in there. And thank gods it's Frigg's-Day, of course. TGIFrigg.

Chapter 14.

THE MAN IN THE MOON

A thing is as immortal as it is young[5]. A short life now, but an endless one.

---

[5] A thing is as immortal as it is young. For instance, the unnamed entity ($\rightarrow$.000001) that came into being first, after the Big BANG (BB), will exist until the same amount of time (the time between BB and first being created) before the End of the Universe (.0000001 $\leftarrow$ ∞ (*oh, look out!*)). The first created, live the longest. The more recently created beings will not last nearly so long, since their end will be just as far away from The End as from The Beginning. But each end of Being, reaching into the past and into the future, approach their beginnings and their endings by getting closer to them at an infinitely fractional rate - they can never quite reach their beginnings or ends. So, no matter how much time passes, they will always be in the exact

When this story began, there was a *very* young entity, just recently created. It came into being only 21 years ago. It was a *truly* miraculous birth. A god born of no gods at all. No divine help, as it were, to conceive.

This god was born of a human couple, very much in love. It was a baby girl. The couple, of course, had no way of knowing that their child was a god. So they raised her like any little girl who is loved.

You'll think perhaps they should have noticed something about her and deduced her immortal state? But she grew and aged like any child. True, she did seem to be the most *beautiful* young

---

center of their time. Days, weeks, months, millennia, circles of time getting smaller and smaller at an infinitely fractional rate, trying to find their beginnings and ends, which haven't happened yet, or ever will. In other words, infinity doesn't reach out, but in.

girl in the universe, but that must just be good genes (they didn't know what genes were back then, but that was the general thought).

And yes, she was extremely clever and confident, but isn't every child, in their own way?

It was a lonely piece of country that they lived on. Not another soul but the three of them for *miles*. And parents can't be with their child *always*. The girl was sometimes all alone. But she didn't really mind. She *liked* to sit by herself sometimes and think up knotty thoughts. Sometimes she would think *such* knotty thoughts, she didn't know how to explain them! Her parents liked to talk with her about them (they loved to actually) but they didn't *always* have the answers. And she wouldn't *always* listen to them, because she wouldn't trust any thought in her head until she had figured it all out, all by *herself*.

When that happened, when there were *no* answers to be had, she would ask The

Man in The Moon, and he would help her understand.

You're a clever one - doubtless you've gathered that this immortal being, born of humanity, is our very own Persephone, the nameless lady!

And Hades went and crowned her a god, all over again! Persephone is more than a goddess now... She's a goddess *and a half*.

If Hades is now puzzling over the lady's strange behavior, he is right to. She knew somehow that she could do *so many things*, but she didn't know how, or where to begin. She didn't have anyone to help her understand things now she couldn't see the Moon, but the possibilities were endless.

If you pass the cavernous dining hall around 2 on a Thor'sday MRT (MORTAL REALM TIME), you'll observe the lady levitating objects with her mind. Nothing heavier than a pencil yet, but you've got to admit, that's not too bad for starters. She had tasked herself with learning more and more of what she could do nearly every hour she was awake. Sometimes even while she dreamed.

Her powers didn't extend to everything. That is to say, she wasn't *good* at everything. She would admit herself that she wasn't good at *lots* of things. Not that she *couldn't* figure it out; if she was stubborn enough about it, she *would*. But *those* things just weren't *her* things. *Some* things were *her* things. That's just who she happened to be.

She was as delighted as she was despondent that *Maximilian Asterisk* had walked into her life, however briefly. Even more so now that she knew he'd loved her too. The Sweet and the Sad of it clung to each other as they spun through her whirling mind.

Although she'd never seen him before and hadn't even known his name, she had recognized him the *moment* she'd seen him. And what bliss, what a sensation!

He was her Man in The Moon.

No question.

And even if she never saw him again, even though it had only been for moments... he had come so *close* to her! So *close*.

And he was still out there - somewhere. Even if she never found him again...

Then again, never's a very long time.

Every day she wished she'd taken that sandwich from his hand. 'One should never turn down a sandwich,' she promised herself every night just before she closed her beautiful eyes to Dream.

Chapter 15.

THE REALLY, REALLY SECRET PLAN

As Persephone dreamt in Hades, and Maximilian tried to find his Way in Valhalla - Hermes was back in the mortal realm. Still onboard the *Undiscovered Express*, he was joined in the dinner car (at the beautiful bar), by his son Pan, and Bert the brakeman. They were hunched over the bar, elbows well in. Their faces were close together. They meant business. They had met there to concoct a genius plan to rescue the fair Persephone from Hades (G.P.). Above them, tacked to the front of the bar, was a sign that Bert had made. It said, *'We're planning The Great Escape'* in a friendly scrawl.

Hermes, as senior here, was leading the discussion of the genius Plan. 'Thank you for being here, gentlemen,' Hermes began with a low but businesslike voice, 'The purpose of our meeting is, I think, already known to us all. The less said, the better, as the nature of our business here today should be regarded as clandestine, top-secret, and all around hush-hush. Higher ups on either end of this business should under no account be informed by either direct or indirect means of our intentions. This means, tell *no one*. Not a soul in Hades, not Zeus, not Hera, not the odd Muse or nymph - *no one*. We don't want any surprises as we conduct this, I may say, high-risk enterprise. No bad guys interrupting us, and no good guys interfering and spoiling our game. Let us agree, before we proceed any further, to swear to a silence *absolute* beyond this circle about *anything* said here today.'

Pan and Bert solemnly agreed, and the three of them shook fast hands.

'Grand.' Hermes continued. 'Then let's get down to business. First things first,' he looked up and grimaced, 'I think we ought to discuss the sign.'

'A sign of *what*, Herm?' Bert asked in a hushed voice, ready to participate. Hermes paused.

'Not *a* sign, Bert,' although he carried himself like thick-set cockney gangsters would eventually, Hermes was always gentle with Bert. 'Sorry Bert, I didn't mean a *sign*. I meant this sign, this sign here, the one you made for us.'

'Don't mention it, Herm,' Bert was honored to be so singled out.

'Well. It's a very nice sign. Wouldn't you say, Pan? A very nice sign?'

'A *very* nice sign, Da,' Pan agreed, 'You have lovely handwriting, Bert.'

'I don't like to brag,' Bert looked down, this was just all so sudden, such fame among gods.

Hermes got ready to be the messenger again. It's a tough job sometimes. 'Thing is, Bert,' Hermes stood and went behind the bar, procrastinating, 'Thing is Bert

(I'll fix you a coffee, Bert), thing is, nice sign as it is... I think that we ought to take it down.'

Bert was horrified that he'd done something wrong! Hermes and Pan *assured* him that he hadn't done anything wrong. And yet,

'Busy platform here, Bert,' Pan offered, 'We don't want to be announcing our plans. Your sign *beautifully* expresses our intentions. And yet, that just, *beautiful* clarity, is the very thing that betrays the sign's presence here, and consequently our subversive and secret undertaking. If that weren't the case, I'd leave it pinned up here *all* the time, if it were up to me. Every day it'd be hanging there - Look at it,' he read it again as a connoisseur, '*We're planning The Great Escape.*' It *exactly* conveys our underground activity, with not a thing left over. It's a thing of elegance.'

'Not so fast son,' Hermes interjected here, 'Nice sign as we all agree it is, I wouldn't say it exactly conveys our objective. We're planning more of a great *rescue*, than a great escape I'd say. That's more like the right word, isn't it?'

'You know what, you're right,' Pan nodded, 'It's *her* escape, but it's *our* rescue. Don't you agree, Bert?'

Bert did, feeling a fool.

'It's important we're on the same page here, boys,' Hermes continued in his low, businesslike tone, 'We're planning a rescue here, but I don't want to hear that word bandied about. I want you both of a mind that this (rescue) is a bit of *errant thievery*. We're dangerous, passionate rogues. You don't want to go around being too *moral*. It puts people off, and it's not as much fun.'

Pan and Bert agreed without hesitation, 'but,' said Bert plaintively looking at the erroneous sign, 'we've got to call it *something*, Herm, don't we? What we're doing, I mean? It's *important*. It's got to have a name.'

Hermes knew Bert was more disappointed than he was even letting on about his sign not working out. He didn't believe in saying *no* to good intentions; that just wasn't his way. So Hermes knocked the bar and said, 'You're gods-damned right, Bert, it's *got* to have a name. And anyone who could make a sign as nice as yours is *just* the one to name it. Can you think of anything as catchy as *the great escape*, but which doesn't give anything away? We need a top-secret code name for history to remember... without remembering us. What do you say, Bert?'

Bert thought hard, and after a few false starts, he said, 'how about *the really, really secret plan?*'

It was unanimously agreed.

Bert, all grins, wrote on the opposite side of the sign, *We're Planning The Really, Really Secret Plan*. Then the three of them hid it away in an empty bottle at the back of the bar so no one could ever read it. The plan was *that* secret.

And that seemed like a good place to stop.

They didn't have a plan yet, but they had a great name.

Somehow... by executing their yet-undiscussed *Really, Really Secret Plan,* they would, by extravagant maneuvers unknown, ~~rescue~~ rob the lady from Hell as only Princes of Thieves could. There might be a big, dramatic chase. There might be explosions. Who knows. Autolycus hadn't even got to town yet, and when it comes to errant thievery, he was one of the *best* for sheer audacity and style.

Whatever the plan worked out to be, they knew one thing for *sure:*

They were going to be badass.

Chapter 16.

A TALKING HEAD

Meanwhile, in Valhalla, Odin had a plan of his own, and he didn't care who else liked it. Which was good, because none of the other gods ever *did* like it when Odin decided to consult Mímir.

He had gathered those present at their new guest's arrival - Frigg, Freyja, Freyr, Loki, and of course Max - in his personal study. This was a rather self-aggrandizing room. There was a portrait of Odin nearly too large to take in all at once. There were skulls and antlers and skins of monstrous creatures he had killed on every surface.

He had poured his guests mead in gigantic cups carved with scenes of terrible destruction, and had sat himself behind a truly massive desk. His desk, contrary to the rest of the room, had almost nothing on it except a carved raven that bobbed continually for water if its tail was touched. Also, a massive knife stabbed deep into the desk's top, and a picture that only he could see of nymph posing seductively next to a great, horned ram with an enormous beard.

As he sat behind this desk now, he stroked his beard, and addressed the company, '*I suppose you're wondering why I called you here,*' he began in his booming voice. '*Each one of you was present at the arrival of our new friend Maximilian. An event I know I'm not alone in thinking, is pretty weird.*'

The room nodded in agreement, Max most of all, now perched on a poof far too large for him, made from the exoskeleton of The It's Just Too Big Nightmare Scorpion.

Odin continued, '*With all of you as my witness, I propose to question...*' he paused for effect, '*Wise Mímir's head! About what should be done.*'

Groans from the room. Frigg stepped up, 'I forbid you to bring out that disgusting, useless head in front of guests.'

'*Well*,' said Odin, aloof, '*Then how about you tell us what we should do then, Mrs. I-can-see-the-future?*'

Frigg rolled her beautiful eyes and sat back down with a queenly *harrumph*.

'*That's what I thought.*' Odin smirked, triumphantly producing the sticky, decomposing head of Mímir from a pocket of his cloak. He held it high for a moment so all could see, and then he sat the head on his desk, facing him. '*Mímir, my friend, it's good to see you -* ' Odin rumbled, ' *- what's that you say?*' he asked the head, '*aw. He says it's good to be seen,*' Odin translated for the rest of the room.

Maximilian wasn't unduly worried about this behavior, but he did want to be clear about it. 'Excuse me,' he said, 'Can we not hear Mímir too?'

The lord Freyr laughed, chagrined, 'No, we can't. We have to take Odin's word for it that that rancid head says anything at all.'

'*I gave my eye to hear him speak!*' Odin stood in a rage, '*What did any of you ever do but* kill *him?*'

Freyr retorted, 'be fair now, you'd killed my sister three times already.'

'*I guess that's fair!*' Odin raged and then sat down, immediately amicable again.

Freyja, the thrice-killed goddess mentioned, brought Maximilian up to speed in her bouncy and ever-cool way:

Mímir had once been the wisest of the Norse gods; they called him, 'the great Rememberer.' He had always been a great (if unlikely) friend of Odin's.

Back in those days, the gods were divided into two different houses - the Aegis and the Venir. The Aegis were a...

physical bunch, apart from Mímir; they were led by Odin, even then.

The Venir were a much gentler and more knowledgeable family. Freyja had been their leader, although back then she was only a goddess of love. The two families each chose among the slain Vikings, half by the Valkyries to come back to Valhalla, half by Freyja to come back to her Great Hall in the realm of Fólkvangr.

When Frigg first announced the prophesy of Ragnarök, End of Days, Battle of the Gods, things changed. Each house wanted *more* valorous slain than the other family - they wanted to make their armies strong against each other in preparation for the Great Battle.

Quarrels inevitably erupted, and attempts for a truce failed miserably; so the next thing anyone knew, Odin was hurling spears at the Venir across his great hall. Freyja was executed not once, but *three* times for leading the charge against Odin.

Her three resurrections in turn created the tremendously powerful goddess of war, sex, love and death, (humbly) telling this story. Freyja eventually forced an alliance with the Aegis. In part, she accomplished this by severing Odin from his one wise friend, Mímir. Literally.

Freyja had cut off Mímir's head rather mercilessly (but she *had* just been killed *three* times, she half-apologized.) Without council, the Aegis were forced to accept the terms of the Venir.

Odin was utterly despondent at the loss of his friend. So much so, he tore out one of his own eyes and sacrificed it down the deep well of wisdom that Mímir had owned. By this rash act of grief, Odin claimed that forever after, the disembodied head of Mímir would still speak wisdom and council to him, and him alone. He carried the decaying head with him everywhere, concealed.

Naturally, the other gods thought this was disgusting. Frigg, his wife, found it especially odious. But nothing could tempt or threaten Odin to put to rest the rotting head of his friend Mímir, once and for all.

And here we are.

'*Shall I* continue??' Odin impatiently asked, '*I'm tired of all this - oh, what's that you say, Mímir?*' Odin listened to the mute head and laughed, '*Yes, I agree,*' he said at length, and said no more.

'...What did he say.' Freyja knew she was being set up.

'*He said that color doesn't suit you, Freyja. It makes your skin look like that of a rotten banana. Ha, ha.*'

'He can't even see me,' Freyja snorted.

'*You don't know what he can see. He can see lots. Tell them Mímir,*' Odin paused, giving the silent head audience, '*So there.*' Odin concluded.

Loki agreed, 'you can't argue with that.'

True, they could not. Nor could they argue with what Odin then said that the head said, '*Mímir says that he has been listening all along, and the story of Maximilian here and the nameless lady reminds him of the prophesy of - what's that Mímir? ...He says it reminds him of the Prophesy of* Ragnarök! *- come again Mimir, my friend? He says - yes... yes, I'd forgotten that...*' Odin listened, rapt, for a time, leaving the room in silence.

Loki spoke up, '*What, for goodness sake!?*'

Odin composed himself and the other gods sat forward. Anything concerning Ragnarök concerned the fate of them all. Odin was pleased to finally have the strict attention he'd been looking for, so he dragged things out a bit to punish them, '*I had forgotten,*' he said casually, '*As you know, Loki here fathered a great snake that he had the bad taste to name Hugemonster. Because it was an atrocity (Loki), I threw it into the great ocean surrounding Middle Earth. It has grown so large that now the terrible serpent has wrapped itself all around the world, holding its tail in its mouth like a baby sucks his thumb. When Hugemonster releases its tail, Ragnarök will begin. The end of days. Many of us will be slain by each others' powers. Loki's other monstrous son, Fenrir the great wolf, has been prophesied to slay me, greatest of the gods - but we'll see about that... I had not thought beyond this prophesy - there didn't seem to be much point.'*

'Yes,' Loki steamed, 'we *will* see about that. But what about this man and the lady, you... bag of... leaking... foul wind!'

'I was getting to them,' Odin was always pleased to ruffle Loki, *'Mímir, my wise friend, reminds me that after The Battle, the mortal world will flood and drown all those who live there. After the floods slink back to the oceans and rivers and lakes, there will be one man and one woman left to re-people the realm.'*

'... Is that *it*?' asked Frigg incredulously, 'I was the one who told you *that*.'

'What's that Mímir?' Odin asked the head and then addressed Frigg, 'Mímir says 'use your imagination, harpy,''

Frigg gasped, 'he did *not* just call me harpy! It was you, wasn't it, you *swine*!'

'Oh no, it was Mímir, I *swear*,' Odin pulled the head closer to himself for safety, '*what's that Mímir?*' Odin listened again, he looked like he was trying hard to remember. '*Right*,' he continued, '*he says that if Maximilian is the man foretold to us, it would explain his presence here. And if Maximilian here is that man, we must reunite this couple and protect them at all costs, for they are the chosen ones to recreate our world. But Mímir, humble head that he has always been, admits he cannot Know this. He says, since Frigg will not tell us (cough), we must take Maximilian to the tree at the center of Asgard which connects the twelve mighty realms. There, we may ask the great dragon who lives within the tree, ancient Malicestriker, for advice.*'

The room could not argue with this. None of them had thought much of what would happen *after* the Great Battle. Like great Odin had said, there wasn't much point when it wouldn't affect any of *them*. But should they ever smash the world to pieces, they would like to see it recreated. Maximilian wasn't the sort of man they would have imagined to be the one who survived the End of Days. But they had all seen *lots* of things happen which they had never imagined could happen. And those were just the things they *had* seen, meaning there must be many more they *hadn't*.

It was agreed that they would travel to the tree at the center of Asgard with Maximilian.

As they departed Odin's study, Maximilian asked Loki, 'did you really name your child Hugemonster?'

Loki took Max by the arm, 'his mother, Angrboða, was a wonderfully sad giantess. You can't help but want to make love to so much sadness. A mountain of sadness. But she smiled when she gave birth to two of the children we had together. Beautiful babies, they both were. She named our serpent Miðgarðsormr: World Serpent to you. I always liked it, never argued it with his mother; it's got a man-about-town kind of feel. But after Odin threw him into the sea, there was a *lot* of talk about it, and the name Hugemonster just stuck. You see,' Loki added before walking away, 'there's always more to the story than any wise talking head will tell you. Bye for now earthman.'

Maximilian thought he liked Loki, as he walked away. Loki may even have liked Max too, but it's always hard to tell with him... For now, they all went to their respective great chambers to prepare for their trip to the very center of Asgard.

Chapter 17.

STRAIGHT FROM THE DRAGON'S MOUTH

Or,

A BIRD OF A DIFFERENT FEATHER

You may wonder at the ease with which Maximilian has managed his fate so far, with so many inexplicable changes in his path. It bears stating that his behavior has not come with ease, but with a strenuously disciplined code of his own devising.

It helped him to know that so many gods took an interest in his story. One thing is always certain: when the gods take an interest, *something* will happen.

Max made a confident figure as he sailed towards the dragon, Malicestriker. The passionate Norse gods in his company found his calm intriguing. They began to wonder how sincere his love for the mysterious lady may be...

They would *not* question his love by the end of his audience with the dragon.

Nor would they have ever guessed in a million years what he would do.

The adventure had begun simply enough. They had decided to travel together in Freyr's boat, Skiðbladnir, known through all the realms as the Best of boats. It could be folded up like a piece of cloth before and after voyages to fit inside a pocket, and it always sailed with a fair wind.

They had sailed with scattered laughs, some too loud or too sudden. It was not every day they went together to the Center. It can be a dizzying sensation to know you're standing at the middle of your world, all that size to every side. Of course, there's always that much size, but the Center's an event.

They had dressed gaily. Freyja wore her famous falcon-feathered cloak, and her necklace, Brisingamen, of fiery, gleaming torc. Her twin brother Freyr, sat close beside her on the bow; in his thin, loose skipper's duds, he looked every bit the god of pleasure. And he wore his magic sword at his side, which would fight on its own, 'if he be wise who wields it.' Odin and Frigg wrapped themselves in a soft deck blanket made from a pelt of the Sweet Gündersplaticorn. Loki had dressed like a pirate.

The gods had opened up their closets to Max so he could dress for the occasion. He had chosen a black, pinstripe suit that Freyja's husband used sometimes to visit 1940's bohemian circles on middle earth. Her husband, Oðr, was a poet so Divine he was often driven to madness. He would wander away for very long times, without even a word! Freyja doubted he'd ever remember the suit, so she made a present of it to Max. It fit him so well. She thought it made him look like a hero, with that strange blue-black moustache. And his blue-black fedora. Black wingtips. A clean, white shirt. Black vest dusted with old starlight. And socks the color of tomato.

When they banked, it was softly against the fine white sand of an island. This is where the tree grew at the center of Asgard. It was a breathtaking sight. Across the sand, the tree was *massive*, with white bark and silvery green leaves; it covered all that could be seen. Around the tree were four white harts, with antlers sharp as arrows. They grazed from the tree, each from a different side, indifferently.

As the party drew closer to the trunk, they could see a golden eagle resting on a low hanging branch. Its head and eyes swerved from side to side. In the center of the tree-trunk at the center of the realms was a hole, which, despite the calm afternoon sun, was totally and uniformly of blackest black.

Freyja took Max by the arm and whispered, 'that's where the old dragon lives.'

Max nodded grimly. Something about that darkness made him long to see inside, but he felt such distrust of it. Practically a loathing.

They halted their progress a respectful distance from the center. The eagle looked at each of them as they waited in silence and in splendor. At length the eagle spoke, 'Ye gods,' he said in a high, raspy voice, 'ye are known to me: Odin the childish; Frigg the shrill; Freyja and Frigg the incestuous; Loki my crooked, old friend.'

The gods had been taught that there was no understanding the eagle's standards. They bore the eagle's words with patience and bowed heads.

The eagle continued powerfully, 'Before me now is one I do not know. This well-dressed man. A rare thing. Who *are* you?' The eagle demanded of Max.

Max stood tall and never wavered, 'I am Maximilian Asterisk. And who,' he asked, 'are you?'

The gods gasped, and the eagle stared at him and screeched, 'You *dare* ask of one so mighty what they're called?! *The greatest, have no names!*' The eagle shook with very rage.

Max apologized, 'But I've got to call you something. Shall I call you Unnamed Eagle?'

The eagle sputtered and then exulted, 'Yes! Very well! Call me The Unnamed! I, who *only* may speak with Malicestriker, dragon who lives at the center of the realms. I, the *Great* Unnamed! Mwa ha ha ha!'

The eagle had been waiting *forever* for someone to call him 'The Unnamed.' To be more precise, 'The *Great* Unnamed,' but this was pretty close. The eagle had always thought that sounded super *coool*. But you can't just name yourself something like that, no one would go for it. But if someone *else* calls you 'Unnamed Eagle,' well then, dreams come true.

Of course, the Unnamed Eagle was not the nicest of creatures, so his dreams may not be the skittles and beer some might hope for. But they were his own. And his day was made.

He cawed in his high, screechy voice, 'Maximilian of Asterisk, ye are a man of worth. Tell me what I may do for ye.'

Odin answered for Max. He wanted to make sure everyone remembered that *he* was the leader of this expedition. Even though they had come for Max, there'd been far too much of Max already. *Come on now*, he thought in a booming voice. So he told the eagle of Max's plight, and of their suspicions about Ragnarök. Concluded, the Unnamed Eagle said, 'I will confer with Malicestriker,' and he hopped into the black hole.

As they waited for an answer, Freyr said, 'it's going well I think,' and Frigg replied, 'I knew it would.'

Freyja rolled her eyes. They waited then in silence.

When the eagle flew from the darkness he said, 'this man is an abomination. He will now be put to death.'

Wait! Why? The gods cried, and the eagle screeched, 'he is in violation of the current laws of physics. If anyone sees him, he'll spoil the surprise. He must be ended now.' And a firestorm blew up from the sand below the Unnamed Eagle, and it rushed towards Maximilian.

'No!' Max yelled above the firestorm, 'You can end me if you wish! But I must know something first!'

The fire slowed its advance as it flickered and roared.

'Ask.' The Unnamed replied, 'Ye shall be answered and then die.'

'Does she love me?' Maximilian yelled; the fire quite close now.

'*Yes.*' came the reply. Max was over the moon. His heart had the strength of ten men. The fire surged towards him again.

'Then hear me!' Maximilian cried. *Hear him!* The others echoed, and the fire reduced to kindles in the sand near Max's toes. 'Unnamed One,' Max began and the fire flickered, 'The Pigeon has brought me here. As I understand it, that is very old magic. Love brought me to the Pigeon. That's an older magic still. I believe we are destined for more than this end. Please,' Max removed his hat, 'give me a chance.'

The sand continued to smolder. The eagle considered, putting his feathers in place.

At last the Eagle said, 'I will confer with Malicestriker,' and hopped again into the dark.

When he reappeared, he boldly rasped, 'Ye bring luck with ye, Asterisk. Malicestriker has given me authority to god ye. Once godded, ye will no longer be in violation of our laws, and may move freely through all the realms, at will. This is a boon deeply to be desired, 'specially considering your outlaw state. All ye must do in return... is give us that which is most precious to ye.'

The gods watched Max fumble as he said, 'I have nothing of worth.'

'Nonsense,' the Eagle wheedled, 'The most precious things have no worth. This is to be priceless. Give us your love of the lady, and ye will be a god. Ye, will be free, Asterisk.'

Maximilian was steel, 'I cannot give you that,' he said, 'If I gave you that love, I'd never be myself again. I'd rather die than lose the thought of her.'

'Very well,' the Eagle was disappointed, 'then, *DIE!*'

And fire engulfed Maximilian who screamed, 'let the dragon kill me himself and not his nameless mouthpiece!'

And the fire was suddenly gone.

'Ye would *see* Malicestriker?' The Eagle asked perplexed. The rest were puzzled too. 'He is the demon who lives at our heart. Dare ye confront him with your own eyes? The mere *thought* has driven sages mad.'

'You say you see him, Unnamed One. I would see him for myself,' Maximilian replied.

The Unnamed Eagle, shaken, answered, 'I will consult the great Malicestriker.' And he flew into the dark.

When the eagle returned, he flapped to his perch and sat stately, 'He says no,' the eagle rasped.

Freyja stepped forward, 'No we can't see him?'

'Right,' the eagle said, 'No.'

Maximilian stepped forward, 'Maybe there is no dragon.'

The Unnamed Eagle *screeched*, 'Of *course* there's a dragon! Look at the hole! 'Tis black as sin at night beyond the realms.'

Maximilian was unruffled, 'then *why* can't we see him?'

The Eagle raged, 'Great Malicestriker need not explain himself to the likes of you, wretched, ungrateful mortal!'

'You're right,' Maximilian agreed, 'He doesn't have to explain himself to me. I'll go see for myself.'

Max no! The gods cried aloud, but Max leapt into the darkness. And for a time, darkness was all there was as he fell through nothing. But then there was light. And a massive eyrie. Max landed within the nest. It was made of riches, silks and chains and jewels. There were no eagle eggs within. It was very untidy. Surely, no one but the eagle ever came here... ever! Old things. Chipped things, crumpled things, magnifying glasses, bits of food, dead things, tortured things, tortured in boredom, spills and stains. Nothing had a spark of joy for all the eye could see. Max had never seen such a place.

There was no dragon there.

And then the eagle plunged from above, ancient flashing talons and powerful hooked beak. '*Why have ye come here? Why have ye done this?*' the eagle screamed as if in pain.

'Why have you concealed the truth?'

'Why does *anyone!?*'

'This is no life.' Maximilian said - he was not afraid.

'How *dare* ye?' the eagle raged, 'This *life* is *mine*. I will *kill* ye.'

'I will stop you.'

'*Ye cannot stop me!*' but the eagle did not strike. It landed in the eyrie, listlessly. It negotiated a few steps through the mess. It picked up a magnifying glass in its talons, 'I cannot see well anymore,' the eagle said over its shoulder, absently. Maximilian watched him.

The eagle looked at the magnifying glass *so* sadly. '...Eagle eyes.' the eagle softly said and dropped the glass. The eagle turned with majesty towards Max, 'tell no one.'

Max came close to the dangerous creature, 'for centuries, you've been pretending to give the dragon's advice. You hop in here, wait a bit, and then hop out again. An illusion for everyone but you. It must be a hollow thing, all these years, to give your own advice, but to be the nameless eagle.'

'The Unnamed,' the Eagle corrected, sadly smiling in its way, 'is all I ever wanted to be.'

'The *Great* Unnamed' Max said, and with a moment's trepidation, reached out to touch the nameless eagle's head. But just before he could, the eagle shuddered, and wrapped his head beneath his wing.

It was too much.

'Tell them,' the unnamed eagle said at length, 'that I have quelled the dragon's wrath, and have saved ye from your idiotic leap.'

'Tell me,' Maximilian Asterisk countered, 'why you would have killed me at the first.'

'I will tell ye,' sighed the eagle, 'but cannot make ye understand. Some things canno' be told.'

The eagle stretched its talons and its muscles distractedly as it thought. Then it rasped, 'It is against the laws o' the cosmos to be immortal as a mortal. This is self-evident. If ye will not become a god, ye must go to a godless place. A realm where no god has ever dwelt is the only place ye will be safe.

'Not every realm is yet known to me, but it is known there is a god for every realm. There is no godless place remaining... save one. For millennia upon millennia, through the many ages, nothing lived there. And so it was ignored, and forgotten over time.

'But now, life is there. It is not very far away: I have seen it in dream. But what lives there is not our realm's. It belongs to the world of man. To their imaginary children. Made in man's image. They call them, characters. Their lives, are stories.

'Sometimes characters die before their story's over, and they must go somewhere else 'til their story be told again. Man has not taken these into account - has provided no afterlife for them. So, the fallen characters have found their own way, into the one Forgotten Realm. There, they squat on the land that gods forgot. They have named this place, **The End.**

This is the only place for ye to go if ye would live forever, Asterisk. There, and nowheres else - or ye will be in contempt of the laws we must adhere to. If ye stray from there, ye must face *the consequences*.

There is but one means of transport to The End that the characters have uncrafted. It is crude. They call it, The Omni Bus. Ye will board the Omni Bus, and ye will live in The End. That, as characters put it, is the role that ye must fill.

'Go now,' the Unnamed Eagle concluded, 'and never come again.' The eagle flew far out of sight, deep towards the bottom of the tree, cursing under its breath.

Max watched him go, and climbed back through the darkness towards his friends.

Chapter 18.

YES

When Maximilian Asterisk emerged from the tree, his companions were seated at a table having sandwiches. The table setting was extravagant. The sandwiches, pimento and cheese. You get these things when and where you wish if you become a god.

Max had turned down a great deal for his mysterious lady love.

When they spotted Max, the gods gave a rousing shout. They had been so worried, they said. They thought he had been killed, but they weren't about to be next. They hoped he understood.

Max did. He took a chair and helped himself to sandwiches. The gods had made them in his honor, they said. And he was, honored.

They wanted to know all about the dragon. No one had ever seen it before, apart from the golden eagle. Max said, 'it's impossible to describe!'

So Odin leapt at him with questions, '*Is it true it has enormous breasts? Huge breasts, each the size of a woman. A dozen pairs all down her front. They say a man could grasp a nipple in either hand and thrust his way between them all. They say that death is certain for any man who does so, because nothing after can ever compare.*'

Maximilian agreed. He said, 'I've never seen such enormous breasts, each the size of a Valkyrie.'

The companions were enthralled.

Frigg asked, 'Is it true that it breaths green fire that smells like cinnamon and lilies?'

'Is it true it speaks in rhyme?'

'I heard it only speaks in riddles.'

'Are its eyes as wide as shields?'

'Are its talons white as moonlight?'

'I heard they were red as blood.'

'Does its voice sound like the sea?'

'I heard it cracks like molten lava.'

To these questions any many more, Max always answered yes. It was the most beautiful, glorious, terrible thing by the time they finally asked,

'What happened down there, Max???'

They couldn't believe he had entered the tree. It was the craziest, bravest, stupidest thing any of them had seen for an age! He wasn't even armed! Had he learned anything useful? Did the dragon tell him aught about the Prophesy of Ragnarök?

Maximilian answered no, Ragnarök hadn't come up. But he told them about The End. The lords were fascinated.

'But why do you have to go there Max?' the goddess Freyja asked.

'To be immortal as a mortal is against the cosmic rules. That's what the Great Unnamed said.'

'So you're *immortal*, Maximilian!' The party was wide eyed.

Maximilian had only thought it himself as he'd said it aloud! The Pigeon had spoke true.

They shook arms with him and slapped his back and kissed his cheeks for luck.

Freyr took their ship from his pocket. As he unfolded it the wind came fair and sweet. They sailed towards the mortal realm to send Max on his way. As they travelled, they talked about what might be next.

Freyja felt a kindred spirit in Maximilian's nameless lady, most likely now a new goddess of death. She promised Maximilian that she would organize a welcoming party to visit her in Hell.

'Hades,' Loki corrected, 'my little girl is Hel.'

And so she was. Loki had given birth to her, although she shared a mother with World Serpent (HugeMonster), and Fenrir the great wolf.

The girl had taken after her mother in that she was a giantess of such tragic temperament that her skin was a cloudy blue. 'We knew at a glance she wouldn't try to make friends,' Loki explained to Max, 'so we named her Hel. That way people would always be sent her way to keep her company[6]. Her realm is far below that very tree.' Then Loki added helpfully, 'I'll try to find the goat-man you told us all about. I'd like to see a goat-man. And if it comes up, I'll tell him where you've gone.'

---

[6] True, this is where the expression 'go to Hel' comes from. Odin cast her into one of the twelve realms to look after Vikings who had died ordinary, domestic deaths. It bears noting as well, that Odin has a tendency towards casting out Loki's children...

Frigg rummaged through her bag and produced two postcards of heavy papyrus. 'You never know when you'll need to send a note,' she said in her motherly way. One pictured a place called the *Cloud Nine Café*. A large, completely transparent establishment (floors, ceilings, walls & doors) floated in outer space near a beautiful whirlpool galaxy. Inside, seated at a cozy, red booth was a young couple kissing over coffee and sandwiches. Behind the bar, drying a glass, it must have been a god. He was so good looking he was hard to look at, but it was clear he enjoyed the view for as far as he could see.

Max said the card was perfect.

Frigg said she was so pleased, and handed him a feather and ink. There wasn't much space to write in, but he didn't hesitate. In a tall, thin hand, in blue-black ink, Max wrote:

I love you with all my heart. No matter what happens, I always have, and I always will. Love, love, love, -Maximilian Asterisk.

P.S. I love you.

He handed the card to Freyja, 'will you give this to her?' he asked. Freyja wiped her eyes, smiled and promised that she would, tucking it safe into a pocket of her falcon feathered cloak.

The second postcard showed a bakery called *Good Heavens!* Painted in a window read, *How can anything so sinful be so go-od!* Inside, a short, thick-set man was ordering from a young, aproned clerk behind the counter. Behind the bulging customer, a child was stealing a confection from the spotless, rustic display with a look of naughty delight.

This one was trickier. At last Max wrote:

Dear Pan,

I'm immortal now, so place your bets! But I'm breaking the laws of physics, so I'm going to The End by Omni Bus. Please come!

Thanks for everything. Your friend, Max

He gave this card to Loki, who flipped up his eyepatch and said, 'all that thought just for *this*? Well, I'll give it to the goat-man... If I remember.' He folded the postcard unevenly and stuffed it under his tricorn hat.

They were nearly back to earth now. Max felt bitter sweet seeing the trees for what may be the last time.

Chapter 19.

THE RENDEZVOUS

Meanwhile, in Hades, Persephone has been working her magic. She had begun by simplifying the income tax code to a simple 15% of anything over Δ300 grasps[7] a year. Sales tax was 5%. She made sure a minimum wage was put in place, high enough to ensure a full-time deceased could after-live in comfort. She had made sure existing businesses could see themselves through the change by converting a large store of Hades and her personal reserves into a trust for this purpose. She had incentivized philanthropic public works by offering unoccupied public lands at a significant discount if a greater good could be shown

---

[7] A *grasp* is a prehistoric form of iron currency. Eventually adopted by Greece, you might know it as a *drachma*. The literal English translation means 'a grasp.' 1 grasp is worth 6 iron *'obols.'* The literal translation of obol is 'spit.' In other words, 1 grasp is worth exactly 6 spits. That's calling finance like it is.

to be served. Local businesses were opening at incredible rates. Money flowed, and before long, dingy and dangerous alleyways were transforming into charming, narrow streets of flowers, colors, and industry.

The deceased of this kingdom had never been happier. And ample money was coming back towards the government to put to larger uses. Roads, bridges, ferries... The ferryman's toll had been eliminated! The ferryman didn't mind. Between his new salary and new uniform, Char had never been treated better or complimented more. The uniforms had been designed by Persephone herself. She could have been persuaded from the color, but truthfully, it bothered Hades so much, she couldn't help herself. Hades had shouted, 'You've got to be kidding, sweet darling! They're pink!'

And Persephone had beeped his nose and said, 'I *know* that.'

'Well I forbid it. Plain and simple.'

'But you said I could do whatever I wanted!'

'And I mean it, but within *reason*, precious cupcake.'

'But I want it. What's the matter? It's just pink uniforms. Everybody likes them!'

Hades frowned. He didn't like any of this one bit. He was proud of the image he'd cultivated. Fear, death, subjugation... black! Everything had been black since he'd taken over. Plus, even if it *may* be for the better, Hades *never* liked change.

Pink uniforms...?

But she was so very beautiful! And he'd kidnapped her. He wasn't insensible of owing her a thing or two after dragging her to hell.

He hadn't wanted to be here himself! Years back, after he and his siblings had defeated their parents (the Titans) in battle, they had drawn straws for who would be the god of what. Hades, Zeus and Poseidon, being the eldest, had drawn lots for the three biggies: Sky, Earth, and Underworld.

Hades had really been hoping for Sky, it's just the coolest one. Earth and water you've got to deal with all sorts of people and creatures, it's a big mess. In fact, that's why when Zeus pulled the longest straw for Sky, he offered to take some of the pressure off whoever got earth. That's how Poseidon, who drew the second longest straw, ended up with just the water.

How nice for him.

And that just left the underworld for Hades. And this Underworld is so *small*. Most afterlives have loads of realms, but not this one. Nope, just the one realm. There was no room to get judgements and awful punishments in place, so they just let *anybody* in. It sucked.

But *somebody* has to be in charge of the Underworld, and Hades had drawn the short straw. So here he was, with the most beautiful woman in the universe telling him she wanted to put the staff in *p-i-n-k* uniforms. And she was beeping his nose. Even if you're evil, that's hard to resist.

'Okay cutie, sure,' he relented, 'just not *too* pink?'

'Just the right amount!' she purred and whirled happily away to make it so.

She had asked for worse things, Hades thought. Some seemed innocent enough, especially when confined within The Residence. At least no one else could see... She had a very unique style for her time. It was very like what would come to be known as *art deco*. He didn't mind it especially.

As she unlocked door after door for renovation, he'd forgotten he had so much *space*! Or so much junk. But rather than throwing it all out, Persephone was in a process of what she called *repurposing* and *passing on.*

It didn't make sense to Hades. Junk is junk, and where's the good in giving something for nothing?

But no matter what he thought of it, Persephone had hired crew upon crew to clean out and repaint the palace. Cheerful colors, warm and cool. And because the light never shined in Hades, she was hanging what she called 'fairy lights' everywhere. Across the ceilings, in waterfalls, over doors, in trees and windows. She said nothing beats soft lighting. When he countered with how much this was costing, she had said that it made him look so powerful and handsome, and that was the end of that.

Throughout this ongoing process, he had been genuinely pleased to find an old photo of Curby when he was just a horrible, three-headed pup. He thought he'd lost it.

He had *not* been pleased when Persephone ordered Curby a poodle-cut for the snakes writhing in his skin. The barber had left pink ribbons on its necks and tails.

The monster seemed to *like* it; frolicking in his massive, stony lair, chewing on squeaky death-size skeleton toys.

Watching this, gaunt in the doorway, Hades felt betrayed.

Curby was his best friend.

He called the creature, reached up to untie the ribbons, and felt a little better.

Pink, he thought, why pink...

Pink was only the beginning.

Persephone had decided to rename the whole realm.

Nobody liked the name Hades. Except Hades, of course. No, her vision required rebranding. A sign had already been commissioned from Calliope, a celebrated Muse.

Welcome to

The RENDEZVOUS

~River Styx-Side~

Meet You Here.

Persephone knew Hades would *hate* it.
She couldn't wait to show him.

Chapter 20.

OF DEATH QUEENS AND ROGUES

Towards *The Rendezvous*, two separate parties were making their ways, unbeknownst to each other.

The first was eagerly looking forward to *welcoming* Persephone as the new Queen of the Dead. Freyja had organized the expedition to the Grecian Underworld along with two of her closest friends: tall, strong Hathor, Egyptian Lady of the Necropolis who opened the door for souls to enter *The Land of Reeds*, among many other things. She wore upon her head the horns of a beautiful cow, with a red disk of plenty resting between them. And Cacao, a Mayan goddess who resided in their many-realmed afterlife, *The Place of FEARRR*; there, she was the Lady of Chocolate. A very plump, cheerful, bawdy lady; all souls immediately wanted to snuggle into her and sigh.

The second party was at cross purposes with the first. They were intent on *stealing* Persephone away. You've met these gentlemen before. Although, there was one addition to their number that they seemed unaware of. A fly loudly buzzed in the cab with Pan, Bert and Hermes as they made their felonious way to the Underworld.

They had perfected their plan. It was elaborate. But it was foolproof, barring any unforeseen surprises.

At 2:41, both parties were on board the *Undiscovered Express,* scheduled to pull into the At-Hand Central Station at 2:53, precisely.

The clerks, attendants, and porters, all handsomely uniformed in pink with a great many silver buttons, had not noticed that the three ladies handing their tickets over for punching were goddesses. They were all of such varied beauties that most souls tried consciously not to look directly at them. Plus, even when one works between realms, it was rare to see a god, apart from Hermes, anywhere near the train. They all had their own means of transport, frequently bizarre.

But the goddesses were curious to see how this new queen conducted her dead. They were impressed so far. They especially liked the uniforms. They were sipping beers in a booth of the dining car, watching the spacey view and chatting without a care in the worlds.

The (goat) men, as said, were up front in the cab, for privacy.

Apart from the fly on the wall.

'...I told you,' Hermes pinched the bridge of his nose; he was exasperated, 'I was too busy stealing the two-dozen, multi-colored oriental carpets, the magic lamp, and the blasted tented cart *and* fireworks to get a message to Autolycus. *And* the costumes. But I'm telling you again lads, we don't need him for this one.'

Pan, dressed from the waist up as a merchant sailor with tight blue jacket, white shirt, red ribbon tie and a round, flat hat, was also frustrated, 'I *know* we don't need him. The plan's perfect. I'm just saying, *again*, that he's going to be disappointed. This is a job for the history books.'

'Well it's too late now.' Hermes concluded with finality.

The fly buzzed.

Bert, burly soul although he was, was kitted out as a Persian concubine in billowy silken harem pants, a tight blue velvet jacket coyly unbuttoned (deeply enough to show his chest hair), a sky-blue veil hid his face, save his eyes (which were heavily made up), and an intricately jeweled headdress hid his hair.

The veil, they agreed, was what sold it.

Bert demurred, 'let's not fight, okay Herm? Pan?'

Hermes and Pan agreed reluctantly, one scratching his crotch, the other his neck.

'Alright,' Hermes said, 'let's just run through the plan one last time.'

This is the plan: Hermes (Mr. Pink), is playing himself. (That took some explaining for Bert to understand.) The three of them would travel from the At-Hand Central Station to The Residence in the cart Hermes had... procured. A wooden affair tented with tall sheets of red and white striped silk, that once belonged to Scheherazade. When stopped by the guards, Hermes would say, 'Good afternoon, Eric (presumably), my name is Hermes, you'll find I'm on the list.' When the guard demands to know who Pan (Frank Jove), and Bert (Scarlet) are, Hermes will explain that he has ventured far and wide to find a gift befitting the new Queen Persephone. At last, he found the perfect treasure: carpets from the orient, woven to tell the whispered stories of the mightiest stars in the Milky Way, each carpet worth more than ten emerald mines.

But as he purchased them, the lady who had woven them grew desirous to see the new queen for herself. This is Scarlet (Bert). But Scarlet is the concubine of a wandering sea-man, Frank Jove of *Rare Treasures by Jove* fame (Pan). Scarlet is forbidden to be in the presence of other men without him. Frank too, wished to see this queen, so beautiful and good. So Hermes has brought the treasure, the lady and the sea-man, all for the queen's delight.

Of course, the guard will never be able to resist such a story.

Once inside, meeting Hades, Frank (Pan) will be dumbfounded by the king's elegance. He will offer him a treasure he has guarded all his life: a magic lamp containing a genie of great power. But, Frank will warn, the genie can only be seen in total darkness. Frank will show Hades how to summon the genie, but no one else may be present. Perhaps Scarlet could be left with the queen where no men are present? She could show the carpets to her highness.

Hades, naturally, will agree to all this, and rush off with Frank and the magic lamp to a pitch black room. Once they are in total dark, Hades will rub the magic lamp, and Pan will set off the fireworks.

Meanwhile, Bert and Hermes will roll Persephone into one of the rugs, place her in the cart, and drive quick-as-can back to the Undiscovered Express.

Hades, blinded by the fireworks, will never notice Pan absconding from The Residence, where he will... borrow one of Hades' many chariots, and fly directly back to the mortal realm, where they will meet up again, no trouble at all.

What could go wrong?

The fly buzzed in short bursts, like laughter.

They had talked precious minutes after the train had arrived at the station.

They hadn't noticed the goddesses strolling past the window. The ladies were now already happily in a cab, and on their way.

By the time the cart and all the rugs had been unloaded and packed, the goddesses had sailed thru the guards without a bit of trouble, and were already knocking at the red door.

Persephone answered, radiant in gold, 'Visitors!' she squealed, 'such deliciously beautiful guests!'

Freyja, Hathor, and Cacao loved her on sight.

Persephone ushered them excitedly over the threshold and into a salon, and as she did, they chatted.

'I *love* what you've done with the place!' Freyja bounced.

'What made of?' Cacao asked with deep curiosity[8]. The Mayans had made over their realms often. Too often, some maintained. Sand, Marshmallows, Corn... They were onto creating everything from Mangos next, fingers crossed.

Persephone said, 'I'm glad you asked. I struggled weeks with it. This realm was originally made of Time. Everything was done in Time. Now, I've tried my best,

---

[8] Cacao spoke brokenly, you see, because the Maya language is put together differently than the others'; she was still learning the 'universal language,' which, at this time, is ancient Greek. That's because the majority of gods living on the one shared realm (Earth) were the Greeks on Mount Olympus. Greece and Egypt and Scandinavia are close enough together to have a shared history reaching *many* millennia back, so Persephone, Hathor, and Freyja have an easier time communicating. But Cacao doesn't even come from Mesoamerica; she comes from an underworld realm called Xibalba. So although she and her afterlife still have a *lot* in common with the others, you're about to find out how unique her home is. Her speech has been translated here as faithfully as possible, to ensure that she is speaking for herself. The point is, the goddess of chocolate is learning, despite a lot of distractions, and that's one of the best things anyone can ever do.

but it just doesn't seem like there's any way to *alter* Time once you've used it. So I figured, that's alright, I'll just paint it *all* over again. We're in the process of a honey and chameleon Creation.'

As the company sat, and Persephone was at the sideboard pouring long glasses of strawberry cider, the goddesses introduced themselves. Falcon-feathered Freyja began, 'We call ourselves the Death Queen Club. We came to welcome you. I'm Freyja, the Norse god of Love, Sex, Death and War. I come from a place called Asgard. There, we keep the souls of brave Vikings who were valorously slain.'

Hathor followed, 'I am Hathor, come from the land of Egypt. Our afterlife is called the Field of Reeds. It is much like your 'middle-earth,' except it is *ideal*. The worthy dead come to work the fields, and there is always a bountiful harvest. When my son Ra, the Sun, disappears from the earth's sky, he travels through the Field of Reeds by river, on a barge. I ride with him there, as he transforms every night from an old, setting sun, to a new dawn again. It is a very sensual place, but very different from here.'

Cacao frowned, 'Mayan afterlife *very* different... I, Cacao, lady of chocolate. Place I come from called Place of FEARRR!' (You could hear the extra R's in the ferocity of the place.) 'Very dangerous. Enter through cave in Belize. Dark caverns, many miles deep. Then cross river of scorpions. Then go through wild land of matched demons. They called Flying Scab and Gathered Blood, they scratch at you when you not look. Then Pus Demon and Jaundice Demon, they make traveler swell up. Bone Staff and Skull Staff turn you into heap of bones. Sweepy Demon and Stabby Demon wait in dirty places to jump out at you and stab, stab, stab. And Wing and Packstrap lead weary travelers far, far astray.'

'How horrible for the poor souls!' empathetic Freyja jiggled.

'Not finished,' Cacao grimaced, 'If soul survive the wild land of demons, they must enter Court of Gods. Other gods there try to trick souls. Put mannequins in their place. If soul greet mannequin, it is made fun of... forever. Gods invite souls sit down, be comfortable... on blazing hot seats. If soul gets burned, it is made fun of... forever. *Ha, ha* they say, *we got you good, boy howdy.*'

'How sad,' Hathor commiserated.

'Not finished,' Cacao shook her head, 'If soul get through Court of Gods in one piece, it must enter each of the Six Deadly Houses: Dark House, Cold House, Jaguar House (full of hungry jaguars), Bat House (full of rabid bats), Razor House (full of sentient razors, move on their own), and Hot House. That one just flames, that easiest one, last.'

Persephone was not the least judgmental, she just wanted to know, 'What happens if a soul makes it all the way through?'

'Nobody knows. No one made it past razor house yet. That's a *bad* house. It is believed, souls *may* go to one of thirteen Skyworlds, where great Feathered Serpent lives...But nobody knows. You want chocolate? I bring!'

It was evident that sweet Cacao's afterlife was not of her own devising. She only stayed there to try to help the poor souls along, as much as she could. Mostly by being a supremely comfortable shoulder to rest on, and by providing most excellent chocolate. The same as the ladies were moaning over now. It was very, very good.

Hathor broke the yummy noises to comfort Cacao saying, 'Do not feel badly, chocolate lady. You know we make our souls undergo trials as well. They are not as trying as yours, but the consequence is graver.' Cacao nodded, they had spoken of this many times. Hathor explained for Persephone, 'Each soul must give us their heart to weigh. If it weighs more than a feather, we cast it to Ammit, *Devourer of Souls*. Only those of light heart may live everlastingly in the Field of Reeds.'

Freyja smiled with chocolate covered teeth, 'We're not so particular. We just let *everyone* in. But we send them different places. It all depends on how you died.'

'It all depends on how you lived,' Hathor nodded.

'It depends.' Cacao concluded.

'Well not here!' Persephone beamed, 'Everyone's welcome!'

The ladies clinked glasses, 'To the dead, bless their souls.'

***

Meanwhile, Hades was several hundred feet below this party, in one of many basements, with his friends Sleep, Death and the Furies. They liked it down there - it was still all black. They were working on a new song for their band, *Psycho Pump*. Practice happened *fairly* regularly, although it was evident that they all liked the *idea* of the band better than actually collaborating on it. None of them were exactly... collaborative. And they all wanted to be lead singer. Except for Sleep, who just wanted to soft shoe quiet rhythms in sand. He was pretty good! But soft shoe alone, does not a band make.

Practice *never* lasted over thirty minutes; by then the quarreling would reach such volume that someone has said they quit.

Practice had been going on for about twenty minutes now, no music had been played, and tempers were high.

***

Approaching The Residence, with a fair amount of squabbling and a little light bruising, the tented cart containing Hermes, Bert and Pan had reached the guards.

'Name?' A guard demanded. It was not Eric.

Hermes was undaunted, he struck an impressive pose and answered, per the plan, 'Good afternoon. I, am Hermes. You'll find I'm on the list.'

'Yes,' the guard made a tick on his clipboard, 'but who are these two?' he stuck his head rudely through the tenting.

'They're with me, mate,' Hermes coolly replied.

'They are right now, sir, but they're not going with you any farther. This paper here says only you're gaining entrance.'

'Well that was before, and this is now, and I, who am on the list, say we're going in together.'

'Sorry sir,' the guard was firm, and somewhat more intelligent than Eric, 'I have my orders.'

'Now you look here!' Hermes turned dramatically indignant, 'I am the wingéd one! Messenger of the gods! I conduct the dead *here*! I'm a part-time employee. And I'm your king's nephew. I vouch for this pair, so kindly stand aside.'

'I can't do that sir.'

'Well how about this. Suppose, just *suppose*, they had been *hidden* under all of these very expensive carpets, and you didn't know they were there. There's no cause for you to search this cart. You'd have let them through *then*, wouldn't you?'

'I suppose so.'

'Then let's just assume you never saw them.'

'But I have seen them. I'm seeing them right now.'

'No you're not.'

'Yes I am. They're right there.'

Clearly, this was not going to (really, really secret) plan. Pan could handle the pressure, but it was clear to Hermes that

Bert was beginning to crack. He kept fidgeting with his veil and nervously tugging at his headdress. Eyes darting. Palms sweating. *Very* inconspicuous.

It was then that the fly shot out of the caravan and flew straight behind a barracks station. Moments later, an impressively tall gentlemen with a great deal of metal on his breast sauntered from that same direction and over to the guard. 'What seems to be the trouble here?' he demanded.

'No trouble sir,' replied the guard. He did not recognize this man, but it seemed like someone he *should*.

'Then let these people through! Do you think we pay you to stand around all day and talk?!'

'No sir!' said the guard at attention.

Forestalling any further argument, the tall man bent to look respectfully into the cart, 'Hello. My name is General Thanks. I apologize for any inconvenience gentlemen, lady.' (He kissed Bert's hand) 'I hope you have a good day. Drive on.'

'Thanks, General Thanks,' Hermes twinkled.

The cart lurched towards The Residence.

Bert breathed a tremendous sigh of relief. Pan parted the striped tenting to spy on the tall gentleman, but he was nowhere to be seen.

Hermes chuckled, 'You see lads? That's what confidence can accomplish.'

'Confidence, Da?' Pan asked, 'Luck, is what it was!'

'No such thing, me boy. A word to the wise, and mark me. Things work out like they're meant to, no matter what, and *luck's* got nothing to do with it. Confidence now, that's looking life right in the eye, and *smiling*, because you don't mind if it's a little *scared* of you. That's how to live life, boys! With confidence. You don't need luck for a sure thing.'

The cart arrived at the front door, they adjusted their jackets, and they knocked.

*****

Freyja said, 'We didn't know you were expecting more company! I hope we're not in the way?'

But Persephone was elated, 'I wasn't expecting anyone. Isn't it wonderful? Let's go welcome them together.'

The foursome bustled elegantly down the freshly painted foyer.

*****

The *Psycho Pumps* had been rehearsing twenty-five minutes and Death had managed to share a new lyric he'd written, '*Your mom's hot like a jalapeno, She's hot like a fire brand, Your mom's hot like fresh wasabi, She's too hot for your dad.*' The chorus just repeated, '*I can take the heat*' over and over. Then one of the

Furies had screamed 'you can't even compare those three heats, that's stupid. And *brand* doesn't rhyme with *dad*.' That Fury was then bashed, repeatedly, through a scuffed, black wall by Death.

***

'Confidence, lads,' Hermes murmured just before the door opened.

The Death Queen Club was not what they were expecting to see. This was not part of the plan. Pan's role was forgotten as he basked in such formidable charms. He admired them all, but his eyes came to rest on the lady Max had described. He had been imagining nightly what the nameless lady Persephone might look like. His most beautiful visions had been surpassed. She hung in space like the French horn's long, lonely note hangs in the air, triumphantly, because of the beauty it's made from sadness.

Bert's mind was less pleasantly occupied. Bert was on red-alert. This was not the plan. He had *learned* the plan. It had not been *easy* for him to learn the plan. He'd *named* the plan, and this was *not* the plan. He didn't trust himself to improvise. No one had said anything about *improvising*. No, everyone said the plan was *foolproof*, barring any unforeseen events. *This* is an unforeseen event...

Even under all his veils and beads, you could tell that Bert was in an agitated state.

Which is why, before Hermes could make an introduction, Bert totally and utterly caved.

'We came to rescue you!' Bert shouted into the ladies' smiling faces. It made sense to Bert at the time as he explained, 'We came to rescue you, but, although, you're being rescued, *you're* escaping. And although *you're* escaping with us, *we're* not escaping... It's a secret.' Bert concluded.

Hermes marveled, and then sighed. 'Queen Persephone, may I present my friend the brakeman, Bert, alias *Scarlet*.'

Persephone was naturally delighted, 'I'm so pleased to meet you! Do you prefer Bert or Scarlet?'

Bert could only manage to echo '...do you prefer Bert or Scarlet?' in response. He'd gone all the way past high alert to numb.

'Which do *I* prefer?' Persephone smiled, 'Scarlet then. Is that alright?'

'Alright,' Bert echoed.

'I'm Pan,' Pan introduced himself.

'Of course!' Persephone hugged him (Pan thought cold thoughts) 'Hermes told me how you took care of Mr. Asterisk!'

'I did my best' (cold thoughts, friend's girl), 'I've never seen someone so bleeding in love. And I ah, know a thing or two about that, if you take my meaning.'

All the goddesses nodded, 'I'm sure you do.'

Then Freyja turned to Persephone. 'I have a message for you from him, from Maximilian.'

For a moment, the goddess and a half flushed pale. It had never, never once *really* occurred to her that Maximilian was anywhere other than in her heart and mind. Of *course* he was out there on his own. Getting to know other gods and goddesses, and who knows who! It was suddenly strange somehow to think that he was real. 'Here it is!' Freyja produced the postcard from her cloak, and Persephone hugged it.

***

The *Psycho Pumps* had been rehearsing twenty-eight minutes now, no music had been played, and the fight had escalated to two Furies trying to pull out Death's skeletal arms. And while Sleep soft-shoed in the corner, Hades was screaming to no one in particular, '*Release the hounds!! Release the houuunds!!*'

***

Persephone greedily read the postcard and announced to all, 'I have to find him.'

Hermes agreed, whispering, 'Everyone, huddle in. We've come to spring you out of here - but we don't know where he's gone.'

Pan whispered at Freyja, 'you must know where he's gone?'

'Yes! It's a place called The End.' Freyja whispered.

'Then let's go!' Persephone whispered.

'We'll all go with you!' the goddess whispered.

'Where are my manners?' Persephone whispered, 'Hermes, Bert, Pan, please meet Freyja (hey hey), Hathor (how do you do?), and this is Cacao (happy sighs).' Introductions done, Persephone whispered, 'What's the plan, gentlemen?'

'I say,' Hermes whispered, 'Simplest is best. Let's change the plan, gentlemen, good plan though it was. I say, at this point, why don't we all just get in the cart and take the train home! Agreed?'

'Agreed!'

As they climbed through the silk to the rich carpets, Bert said, relieved, 'This is a whole lot easier than I thought it would be!'

'*Not so fast.*' A voice jagged through the doorway. Hades stepped through towards them, 'just where do you think *you're* going?'

Chapter 21.

FOUR ACES ON THE TABLE

Hades was in no mood for hijinks. He hated hijinks all the times, in fact. He wasn't very good at them, and he really resented people who were. But today, after that band practice... he was in *no* mood.

He angrily walked to the cart, reached in and pulled Persephone out. He snatched the postcard from her hand. 'What's this?' Hades demanded, reading it, 'Who's Maximilian Asterisk?'

'The man with the moustache.' Persephone coolly replied.

'And is this who all.. whoever you all are...' he waved absently, smiling mockishly, 'are going off to see?'

A fly buzzed near Persephone. She considered and then, 'Yes,' Persephone candidly concluded.

The rest of the party didn't look like they knew what her play was... But she seemed so *confident*.

'Hades,' Persephone said evenly, 'by the ancient right of the Realm, I challenge you. If I win, I go. If I lose, I stay. Do you accept?'

Hades frowned. He was under no illusions that Persephone loved him. But he *did* love her. And he had never anticipated a formal *challenge*.

How had she even heard about such an ancient tradition?? That was from *ages* before he'd taken over!

But you don't get to be king of the underworld for nothing; Hades had never lost a challenge. So with a saddened arrogance he sneered, 'I accept.'

'Choose weapons,' Persephone said.

'Poker then.'

'Poker it is.'

Hades played a great deal of poker, and when you play poker with Death, you play to win. To his knowledge, Persephone had *never* played poker. And that was true; she never had. This would be a first. Yet she had accepted without hesitation? Hades would have wondered more at this, but why bother? He had already foiled her futile attempt at escape, *and* there was just no *way* she could ever beat him at cards.

Persephone ushered everyone into a room that looked *very* newly decorated. The paint was still wet on the walls. The idea for it had come to her in a dream. They had entered through swinging doors into what looked exactly like an old-timey Western saloon, apart from the pink uniform on the bartender, behind the gleaming wooden counter. The bartender was shooing a fly. He was quite tall and broad with a mane of red hair, and he had a curious scar on his face, just like a question mark. As they entered, he gave them a wink.

Persephone sauntered towards him in a way that befit the room, 'Hi there, mister,' she said, 'say, can I get a deck of playing cards, and a round of whiskeys for my friends? Excepting the fellow in black there. He don't drink.'

'Sure thing, pretty lady,' the barman replied with a professional smile, and with stunning speed, there were the cards and the drinks.

'Say, thanks a lot,' Persephone grinned.

Hades had never seen this room before and said as much, 'what kind of a place is this?' he asked.

'You like it hubby?' This was all that the lady would say, smiling that most cunning smile in the Universe. 'Take your seats please, ladies and gentlemen.'

At the center of the floor was a table made for eight, exactly the number in the party.

Seated, Persephone pushed the cards towards Hades, 'you mix them up please, I don't know how.'

Hades smiled, 'of *course* sweetness,' this was going to be *so*. *Easy*. Hades loved taking candy from babies... 'but just to be sure, why don't we use *my* deck? That way we'll know you're not cheating.'

Persephone looked crestfallen for a moment, '...alright then,' she reluctantly agreed. '...I'll just give these back to the bar.'

'I'll take them,' Freyja bounced up and handed them back to the handsome barman, who placed the cards back out of sight.

A fly buzzed.

The rest of the party was silent, the air was thick with suspense. They all cared what became of the lady. True love was at stake. And possibly the reCreation of an obliterated earth, if one believed the signs of The Pigeon, and Mímir's talking head, and The Great Unnamed eagle. Regardless, this game would determine the fate of two, and consequently, of *many*.

Hades produced a battered deck of playing cards from his pocket. He doubted that he would need to cheat, considering his opponent, but if he needed to, he could. He had memorized every snag, and bend and mark upon them. He shuffled them like a showman and smacked the deck down with finality on the table. 'Care to cut?' he slid the deck towards Persephone.

'Cut?' Persephone asked.

'Cut the *deck*, darling,' Hades couldn't believe how easy this was going to be! 'Just pick some of the cards up - don't show me! (sigh) - just pick some up and set them down next to the rest of them.'

'Alright' Persephone reached for the deck, but before she could touch it, Hermes spilled his drink onto the cards, 'Sorry 'bout that!' Hermes said, wiping his hands.

The barman leapt with surprising agility over the counter with a rag, 'I've got it!' he cried. He picked up the cards quickly but carefully. No one watching could say that a single card's order was disturbed. 'There,' he concluded with a smile. 'I'll get you a fresh drink, mate.' He added to Hermes with a wink, 'Gin this time, so it won't stain.'

When all was reset, Persephone stood, 'Just to be clear friends,' she said, 'The ancient challenge states, that only one try is allowed for a weapon. In other words, today, we will play only one bout of poker.'

'It's a *hand* of poker darling,' Hades sighed.

'...We will play only one hand of poker. If I win, I'll go with the rest of you to

The End to see Mr. Asterisk,' she smiled, 'If I lose, I've given my word to stay here at The Rendezvous.'

'The *Rendezvous?!*' Hades sputtered, 'since when?'

'Barman?' Persephone called, and a pink sheet was pulled from Caliope's newly completed sign:

Welcome to

The Rendezvous

~River-Styx-Side~

Meet You Here.

'If I stay,' Persephone continued, 'this *will* be the name of this realm.' Hades gawked. 'Are you sure you *want* me to stay?' she coyly asked.

'Darling...' Hades said through gritted teeth. Oh, he was mad. Springing something like this on him in front of guests. He hated having guests anyways!

'we'll *discuss* it, *later.*' His mouth barely moved, his eye briefly twitched.

'Alright!' Persephone agreed cheerfully. 'Who should hand the cards out? We want this to be fair and square.'

'Who should *deal,* gorgeous one,' Hades corrected, brightening somewhat. She was beautiful, but my word, she was an *idiot* when it came to poker! *Candy from babies* Hades thought to himself, smirking.

Hermes stood, 'I think it should be someone with the least vested interest. Since we've only just met the barman, and he seems an able sort, I suggest that it be him.'

'I agree to that if Hades does,' Persephone offered.

'I have no objection,' Hades agreed. It didn't matter who dealt when it was *his* deck.

The barman took off the coat of his pink uniform, revealing god-like strength in his arms. He straightened his apron, and solemnly picked up the deck. 'The game,' he announced, 'is Snakeskin. You'll each be dealt five cards. The cards you hold are the cards you're discarding. The cards you show are the cards you're playing. You'll get new cards to replace the cards you show. You'll have two opportunities to change cards. After that, the best hand of five showing, wins.'

The cards snapped as they landed effortlessly in front of Persephone and Hades.

'Ladies first,' Hades said, surprisingly affable. He did love to play poker.

'After you,' she insisted.

Without hesitation, Hades lay down two cards, both kings.

The barman gave him two new cards.

Persephone studied her cards. She hid the cards in her hand. Her face gave away nothing. At last she laid down a two of spades.

A new card was slid to her.

Hades laughed and slammed a third king to the table.

The party murmured amongst each other.

Persephone lay down an ace of hearts.

Hades triumphantly lifted his last two cards on high, and they showed them to be a Jack of Clubs... and the fourth king.

Hermes said, 'The only thing can beat four kings, is a royal flush or four aces, and that ain't ever gonna be a royal flush.'

Pan grimaced, 'It's not often you see four aces on a table.'

Persephone looked blankly at her hand, and without ceremony laid down the last three aces. Four of a kind.

Hades boggled. Then he seethed, 'you've just had them in your hand? Do you even know that you've won?'

'Beginner's luck,' Persephone said innocently, 'you don't seem very happy about it.'

'*Happy?!*' Hades stood up abruptly, knocking his chair over. The company tsked and gasped. 'I'm over the moon. It was a terrible idea to bring you here. I don't need anyone brightening things up. And the only way to change this realm's name is over my dead body! Go! And good riddance. But if I find out you cheated here, I will find you again. I'll bring you back. And next time, I'm not playing nice.'

Hades stormed out of the room; the party watched him go. Then he stormed back in, 'I forgot my cards,' he said as though proclaiming their doom. He gathered them together as the rest watched, and then he exited again.

Bert broke the silence, 'well that was lucky, wasn't it?'

'Luck's got nothing to do with it mate,' It was the bartender who spoke, removing his apron, 'Shall we go?'

A fly buzzed into the room, rounded it as though doing a celebratory lap, and then buzzed away again towards the cart.

'We shall,' Persephone said rising, 'let's go to The End.'

Chapter 22.

CHEAT A CHEATER

They boarded Scheherazade's cart without sight or sound of Hades. Still, something told them all to stay silent till they were well past the guards.

It was the barman who spoke first, 'I'm Autolycus, by the way,' he said by way of general introduction. 'Prince of Thieves. Call me Otto. I'm very pleased to have made your acquaintances, especially yours m'lady.' He kissed Persephone's hand.

'It's bloody good to see ya!' Pan said.

'You too, little brother.'

Hermes was twinkling, 'I think we're safe now, ladies and gents! There's one more introduction due...'

With a whoosh, a fly which had been happily resting on sweet Cacao's thigh, suddenly transformed into,

'Loki!' Freyja exclaimed.

'The same,' Loki jauntily raised his eyebrows, and as he removed himself from smooshed Cacao, he apologized, insincerely.

Bert had gone straight through confused to catatonic.

Hermes explained.

The Really, Really Secret Plan had always been a ruse. It was a plan *meant* to be interrupted by Hades, so an even more secret plan could go underway, undetected. Hermes had long known of the right to formally challenge the king of the underworld. He'd always hoped to be able to put it to use someday. When Loki introduced himself to Hermes back in the mortal realm, while looking for Pan, it seemed too good to be true. A shapeshifter - just the trick.

Persephone had of course been included in all this planning. She had set the scene just so. She'd let Hermes know exactly when to arrive, so they would be interrupted in the act of escaping; Hades practiced at almost the same time every week, and it *never* went over thirty minutes.

She hadn't known that the Death Queen Club would arrive just before, but as Hathor offered, 'some things just work out happily.' All the Death Queens agreed, they wouldn't have missed this for a *world*.

When stopped by the guards, Loki had always been ready to fly interference as 'General Thanks,' and a good thing too.

Otto had arrived the day before, to be fitted for his uniform, and stand ready at the bar.

Hermes and Otto had correctly guessed that Hades would choose his strongest weapon - cards.

Although, originally, the cards that Persephone had requested from the bar were already *Loki* in the shape of a deck of cards. They hadn't counted on Hades wanting to use his own deck. Which is why Persephone thought quickly enough to return the deck to where no one could see them change shape again. And Hermes thought fast too, spilling his drink on the new deck. And Autolycus, Loki in hand, expertly switched Hade's deck for the Loki deck while drying them.

Pan agreed, 'you're right Da. You don't need luck for a sure thing. Just one question. Why didn't you let me or Bert know about this? You could have trusted us!'

Hermes agreed, 'I trust you to the very end, me boys. But you'd have never agreed to the costumes. And you just look so bloody adorable! Ah! 'Tis a father's dream.'

Pan tossed the round sailor's hat at his Da.

'Ah now. It's a good day,' Otto sighed, 'It's not often you see four aces on a table.'

'Not unless you cheat.' Loki beamed.

They were pulling into the At-Hand Central Station. Home free.

'*AHA!*' an invisible voice ricocheted within the cart, '*I knew you'd cheated!*'

And then, removing a black helmet, Hades became visible, sitting in their midst.

'You thought you could get away with it, didn't you?' he growled, 'they don't call me king of the underworld for *nothing*.'

Bert was still beyond confused, 'When did you get here?'

'I have always been here!' Hades snapped, 'Wearing my helmet of invisibility.'

Hermes laughed, 'Honestly... What kind of a *god* needs some dumb gimmick like a helmet of invisibility?'

'I dunno,' Hades sauced, 'What kind of a god needs sandals with wings?'

'...Touché.' Hermes conceded.

'Enough of this!' snarled Hades, 'You cannot cheat me of my bride. She returns with me now. And you are all banned from this place. Forever! That is final.'

'Hold on now,' Otto interrupted, 'Can you *prove* that we cheated?'

'You all just confessed!'

'Yeah, but where are your witnesses? It's just your word against all of ours. And I say she won fair and square.'

That's right, yeah! From the rest of the cart.

But Persephone's voice rose above them all, 'he's right.' She said. She looked through the silken tent at the

Undiscovered Express. It was only twenty steps away... But she continued, 'Hades cheated me of my old life. But if I cheat to escape him, I'm no better. I'm sorry,' she looked to all her new friends, 'I'm sorry to have put you through so much trouble. It was a very good plan. But I shouldn't have agreed to it. I just so wanted to see... Maximilian Asterisk. I love him.' She looked Hades in the eye, 'I always have loved him, even when I didn't know him; and I always will. No matter what you do with me. Keeping us apart doesn't change anything. I do not love you. I will never love you. And the harder you try to keep me here, the harder things will be for you. Know that, and I'll come freely.'

Hades scoffed, 'Come then, Queen of Hades.'

'Queen of The Rendezvous,' she corrected. She kissed each of her friends softly, climbed down through the silks, and walked, without Hades, into her streets of happy subjects. Just before turning a corner, the goddess and a half looked back to them all, smiled the dearest smile in the Universe, waved at them, and disappeared.

Hades didn't know how to make a graceful exit. So after watching his queen disappear, he turned to the company remaining and snapped, 'try anything like this again and you'll be locked up with the Titans in Tartarus before you can say Cyclops. So *there*.'

And he tripped over his cloak climbing out of the cart, and pinched his finger, which he sucked, and blustered away after the Queen.

The rescuers marveled. 'We've *got* to get her out of here.' They agreed. 'We can't let that sweet lady stay with such a giddy prick.'

So saying, they travelled the last few steps of the journey and climbed aboard the train. They didn't know how, or what it might mean in the big, *big* scheme - but they were going to rescue her, and reunite her with Max.

Chapter 23.

THE END

Maximilian had left his friends where Persephone had left him. He had leapt from the boat as it sailed just a few feet above the ground, leaving the Norse gods to sail on without him. They had all promised to visit him, and he was very grateful.

Now for the first time since he'd seen the lady, Max was all alone.

Looking about, he saw the yawning hole of blackest black still standing. He went to the very, very edge. *She* was somewhere down there, where Max could never go. He sent the nameless lady all his love, unseen.

He hadn't thought, till the time had come, that he did not know where or how to call the 'bus' the eagle spoke of. But it came to him in a flash, like he had picked up a radio signal: 'And they lived happily ever after,' Max proclaimed into the air. And he was right. Out of nowhere, the Omni Bus was there.

It was constructed from some kind of green metal. Or maybe that was just rust. It was very long and thin. The windows were all darkened, it was impossible to see in.

With not a soul around him, Max took his courage to him, and approached.

The door swung open with a grating creak.

'Get innn already,' the bus-driver groaned. It was a pretty, young woman, who looked in no mood for anything. 'Come onnn,' she continued, 'you're my last stop before The End. I haven't got all day. Just get innnn!' she was clearly at the end of her rope.

So it was that Maximilian Asterisk boarded the Omni Bus, without ceremony, tripping up the steps and into

what he could now see was an empty
bus, save for one.

'Hey guy!' the passenger hollered, 'come
sit with me, huh?'

Maximilian did. The bus pitched
forward and through the windows, the
trees vanished and became blackness.

'Don't mind her,' said the passenger in
sotto voice, 'She's one of the *always*
dead.'

Max looked blankly.

'You know,' the passenger continued. He
was a thick set, balding, regal looking
gent, 'the *always* dead. The ones that are
dead when their story begins! You
know...'

The passenger seemed at a loss that Max
wasn't understanding this.

'You know, like: you've got your cute
orphan kid. They talk about their mom
and dad that were never there. How good
they were, or what bums they were, you

know... The backstory. *She's* one of the always deads. When her story starts, someone's *already* massacred a bunch of whoevers in a castle - she's one of them. Her story *actually* starts with some mook looking for revenge. It's always revenge these days. There's like a ton of these always-deads. Man, they had it rough until we found The End. They didn't have *no* where to go.

'No surprise they're all pissed the funk off. It's like the people who created them just had no idea, you know? Sometimes I look at stories and just think: How is *this* part of the *plan*...?'

The passenger scoffed. 'I'm Oedipus, by the Way. Call me Eddie. Eddie Rex, Eddie the King... you know, whatever suits ya.'

He bore himself like a late twentieth century construction worker.

Max asked, 'You're a king?'

'Nah,' Eddie replied, 'I just play one. It's messed up man.'

Max blinked his confusion, 'what's your story?'

'You wanna know my story? All right man, but stop me if you've heard it. I'm pretty popular right now, you know what I mean? So there's this plague in my kingdom. So, no problemo, I send my brother in law, Creon to go check out what's happening with the Oracle. He comes back and says, *'oh no, someone killed the king before you, we gotta figure out who it was and punish 'em, and then the plague will go away.'* I say, 'no prob.'

'I call this *other* fortune-teller guy to come tell me who killed the king. And he's all, 'Oh it was *you*, man.' And I'm like, 'no way, I'd remember that, right?!' and he's like, 'No, it was you, and you're gonna marry your muddah, and you're gonna kill your Pops, and you're gonna wind up blind and wandering around till you *die*.' And I'm like, whatever, I'm already married to this smoking hot broad. Why'm I gonna leave her to marry my Ma? It don't make no sense.

'So I tell my wife, and she's all, 'don't you believe no fortune tellers. I had one tell me that I was gonna marry my son, and he was gonna kill my husband, and none of that shit happened.' So I'm like, 'right?! Alright then.'

'But I send a message to my Ma anyway, and I'm like, 'just so you know, I'm never gonna marry you or kill pops,' and the messenger comes back and he's all, 'they don't know what you're talking about. But just so you know' (the bonehead says like he's being helpful) 'just so *you know*, they're not really your parents. I was the guy the brought you to them after I found youse as a baby who was cast out of *this* kingdom.'

'And I'm like, 'oh no!' and I tell my wife, and she's like 'oh *hell* no!' and freaks out. She's runnin' around, she's crying.

'It turns out, my wife *was* my mother, and on my way back into the kingdom, I *accidentally* killed my old man while I was rolling with some bandits. So the prophesy *was* true all along. And then my wife, aka Ma, hangs herself, and I gouge out my eyes with pins from her dress because I just can't stand it no more. There's more stuff, where I'm like, with my daughter, and I've got magical powers, but then there's like a *sign*, and I'm like, 'it's my time,' and I lay down and die.

'That's my story.'

Maximilian liked Eddie.

And it was just as his story concluded, that they arrived at their destination.

There was a rough sign, made of some cast off shoon that must have been lying around. Handwritten upon it was:

You've reached

THE END.

~here be no gods~

Max and Eddie disembarked, waving polite goodbyes to the not so polite bus driver. Max looked all about him. It was grey; sketchy. There were many characters there who didn't seem to be... finished. Childish characters who had been murdered brutally, or comically, had erected two-dimensional huts in what seemed like a rough area. The characters there were sleeping, or begging, or raving.

There was also a more sophisticated area, where blurry chandeliers hung from somewhere *far* up in the sky out of sight, and chaise lounges, and billiards, and black and white paintings hanging on the air. But the characters there seemed to be popping in and out of existence. One moment there, the next gone. These characters had firm, elegant edges, but they were still colorless.

As Max wondered at it, Eddie said, 'Sayyy, don't tell me you ain't never been here before?'

Max shook his head.

'Well welcome!' Eddie cheered, 'to The End. We made this place ourselves. It ain't much, but it's ours. Ain't no gods here to bother us, and no men coming to correct us or interpret us... Rules is simple. Don't frickin' bother nobody, and nobody'll bother youse.'

Max agreed.

'Say,' Eddie continued, 'I got nothing but time to spare here. You wanna tell me *your* story?'

And Maximilian did.

Finished, Eddie said, 'Hey that's some good story Max. But I gotta tell ya... That don't sound like no book or no play. Who was it, you said, who wrote you?'

'No one. As far as I know.'

'So that makes you one o' *them!* People! And you say the gods pushed you here, just like the people pushed us?? Yeesh. Well, you're welcome here as far as I'm concerned, buddy. No problemo from me.'

Maximilian was glad.

'But I ask you this, Maximilian: If that's true, you got no more story left to go to.'

'Not if I have anything to say about it.'

'Gutsy, hey, gutsy. I like it. But, in the meantime, while you try to find your lady love, what exactly will you *do*? You got no other story to go to.'

'Then I'll listen to yours.'

'I ain't gonna be here all the time. I told ya. I'm popular. I die *all* the time.'

'Then I'll listen to theirs too.'

'You're crazy,' Eddie Rex concluded. 'But if you *wanna* listen, I tell you what really bothers me, like, all the time, is the lady who's my ma. Why'd she get rid of me in the first place? If she hadn't, none of it would have happened. I could be living the sweet life. I guess you don't know this, but the characters that don't die, just keep living their lives, between the lines. They hang out. They've got a home base. They don't gotta go away and wait for their story to get told again. They got it *easy*. And my ma took that from me.'

'Her character did,' Maximilian replied, 'she's not your mother any more than you're the king now. Isn't that right?'

'Yeah, I guess so.' Eddie was hesitant. 'But if that's true, then don't that mean, that I've been harboring resentment against her for decades for no reason?'

Maximilian didn't know.

'You know,' Eddie said, 'You're alright. You're like a horror character I met once, he was written to look after dead guys... whaddya call 'em... they figure out *why* folks died?'

'A coroner,' Max said.

'Yeah that's right. A coroner. You'll be like a *storybook* coroner. That's what you can do here. We got a lot of questions and resentments and fears here that need examining, you know? Like, objective assessments?'

Max is the sort of man who enjoys doing things that you can really *do* something about. So he agreed without hesitation, 'Yes. Until I find the nameless lady, I'll be The Storybook Coroner.'

'Swell. Hey, nice socks! What kinda color d'ya call that?'

'Tomato.'

And so it was, they walked together into the land where Max was to have many, *many* adventures, with many more storybook characters, and gods, as Time turns.

But for now, until you hear from The Storybook Coroner again, know that you'll always see him waiting for his love, every time and everywhere you see:

THE END.